The Amethyst Bride

The Scottish Stone Series, Book Two

Kelsey McKnight

The Amethyst Bride

First Print Edition: June 2017

Limitless Publishing, LLC
Kailua, HI 96734
www.limitlesspublishing.com

Formatting: Limitless Publishing

ISBN-13: 978-1-64034-123-4
ISBN-10: 1-64034-123-4

Dedication

This one's for all the readers of *Queen of Emeralds* who craved the next installment. It's also for the last of the MacGregor clan, the ones who lost on the battlefield with the Jacobites and again in the years that followed. *Àrd Choille!*

A special thanks to my editor, Rosa Sophia, who probably knows my books better than I do. And also to my author BFF Sarah Fischer who loves Penelope's story and taught me it's okay to have a good ugly cry over a book as long as you can fix your makeup afterward.

The moon's on the lake, and the mist's on the brae,
And the Clan has a name that is nameless by day;
Then gather, gather, gather Grigalach!
Gather, gather, gather Grigalach!

–*MacGregor's Gathering* by Sir Walter Scott

Chapter One

Penelope Elmsly reread the brief note her maid had brought her, the writing in the familiar, swirling style of her best friend, Charlotte Holloway.

My Dearest Penelope,

I know that I am such a horrible friend for not having kept you better informed, but there had been such a turn of events, I feel as if I am in a thrilling French novel.

The horrid Richard Howard came to Scotland in order to take me back to England, I was nearly poisoned by a mad maid, and then Richard managed to kidnap me and almost had me forced into marriage before Conner came to the rescue. Father and Abigail were in attendance and have seen Richard's true form. The tale is too long and convoluted to put into writing, so I will regale you with the full story the moment I see you! But I am pleased to say that I am now to be officially married in the eyes of God, home in England.

Pray, do not be angry with me, for I have taken your advice to heart. I've found a husband who adores me and supports my dreams out of love! I'd like to say it was all thanks to you, but my unladylike ways have been quite the hit here. I'll call on you as soon as I am home so that you can help me plan my wedding.

All my love,

Charlotte

Folding the letter and slipping it into one of her writing desk's many small drawers, Penelope sighed. Charlotte had fled from England in the dead of night to escape a forced marriage a few months before. She had gone off with a Scottish chieftain named Conner MacLeod, and now they were returning to London to have a grand wedding. While Penelope was more than pleased that her friend had found happiness and love, she couldn't help but feel a faint pang of disappointment at her own losses in romance.

She had gone through two London seasons without hearing wedding bells in the springs that followed. Men had flocked to take her on carriage rides and sent her flowers, but her parents had never thought any man was good enough for their youngest child and only daughter. So, the seasons came and went while Penelope crept toward spinsterhood, dreaming of a marriage and children that seemed so far away.

Penelope stood, wrapping her fur-lined robe tighter around her middle and went to the window. The last snows of winter were melting, meaning the spring season of weddings was officially upon them. As soon as the orange blossoms bloomed, florists would be flocking to the countryside in order to supply all of London with wedding flowers. She was starting to hate the mere scent of the dainty blooms.

A dozen new gowns had been ordered for her to wear to all the weddings she was to attend. In the pews of the churches she would feel the eyes of society upon her. “Such a pretty girl. Shame,” they would whisper. “I wonder why she isn’t married?” They would titter behind open fans at the grand receptions. “Perhaps she’s *used goods*!” They would gasp as she left in a carriage alone. The women would all be speculating about why the beautiful heiress Penelope Elmsly could never find herself a husband.

“Dash it all.” She drew her shades shut and rang the bell to summon a maid to help her dress.

She wasn’t sure when Charlotte and Conner

would return from Scotland, but she wanted to be sure to get them a spectacular wedding present. Just because she had been unlucky in love didn't mean she would begrudge her dearest friend a happy life with her husband. To be honest, she was truly happy for Charlotte in all of her good fortune.

Once she was dressed in a forest green velvet gown trimmed in sable fur, she had her hair quickly pinned up and a new hat placed upon her white-gold curls. She admired the velvet and black-feathered confection, which she believed made her cornflower eyes look brighter against her fair skin and rosy cheeks.

She took her purse and called for a carriage to be made ready for her excursion. Her father came down the stairs just at that moment, already dressed to go to work.

"Good morning, darling." Baron Edmund Elmsly kissed his daughter's cheek. "And where are you off to today?"

"I've had word from Charlotte that she's returning to England to have her wedding. I was going to go to the shops for a gift."

The baron pursed his thin lips. "Does her father know of this?"

"Yes, Papa, I've already told you. He is in Scotland with her now, and is in full acceptance of their match. Apparently her previous betrothed wasn't the gem her father thought him to be. I do believe he should be quite pleased as she is marrying into their form of royalty."

"Very well." He didn't make a secret of the fact that he wasn't altogether thrilled that his daughter was the known associate of a girl who had caused such a commotion. But he had known Charlotte since she was very small and he knew the girls were as close as sisters. Still, he had hoped that Charlotte running off with a Scotsman wouldn't ruin her chances of finding a good husband and firmly told Penelope so, many times.

"Are you off to work, then?"

"Yes. Shall I call for a carriage?"

Penelope adjusted her hat. "Already done."

They exited the house together, on their way to the same destination. Edmund Elmsly owned England's first shopping arcade, The Piccadilly Emporium. It was a large building that sold many of the high society necessities—ribbons, ready-made silk dresses, art, hats, furniture, silver, jewelry, and all other manner of fine merchandise. While business had been slow the past two years, as more and more people imported their goods from France, Edmund had still been able to give his children a top education and prepare a handsome dowry for his beloved daughter.

Penelope watched out the window as the horse drawn carriage made its way down the chilly boulevards toward Piccadilly Road. Happy couples walked arm in arm against the cold and ducked into teashops, their chaperones shadowing them at a safe distance. She turned back to her father, who watched her from his seat before her.

"Darling, are you all right?" Edmund asked.

"I'm all right," she lied. "I'm just a bit tired."

"Shall I call for some tea while you shop? You could take it in my office."

"No, thank you, I won't be very long."

He nodded, hands on his walking cane. Penelope had never seen her father without it. Her parents were older when she was born, the surprise child that no one expected but adored nonetheless. Edmund's cane was made of fine wood, topped by the head of a wolf cast in silver. Years of use had begun to wear the metal smooth. It was oddly comforting to have this ever-present cane in sight. But it was also a sign of her father's advanced age. Even now, she could see deep lines marring his once relatively smooth face. The same could be said of her mother, Cecily, although Penelope was wiser than to say it out loud.

Cecily, now a grandmother eight times over, was very pleased upon giving birth to a girl after four rowdy boys. She had invested all of her time in molding Penelope into the perfect society lady. As a result, Penelope was poised, well-spoken, educated, and could plan a lovely party to which all of the ton would hope to receive an invitation. However, Cecily, although she did not voice this thought, took it as a reflection on her parenting that her daughter had not yet been married.

What neither parent would admit to was the fact that they could never agree on which suitor could be allowed to marry Penelope. At least that's what Penelope suspected when each man was sent away. The young heir to a banking fortune cared about his horses too much, so he obviously couldn't appreciate the jewel that was Penelope. Victor Harmsworth, the son of a decorated general, collected weaponry, so of course he would be a violent husband. Christoph, the owner of London's newest railway system was already balding, so his genes were most likely contaminated and all of his children would be born ugly and dumb. Penelope was quite sure her parents subconsciously invented these flaws in order to keep her home as long as possible.

When the carriage pulled to a stop before The Piccadilly Emporium, Edmund exited first, helping Penelope safely to the ground. "Will you be all right on your own?"

"Yes, Papa. I shouldn't be long at all."

He turned to the carriage driver. "Wait here for my daughter to finish her errands."

"Yes sir." The driver tipped his hat.

Edmund led the way into the shop, nodding at his employees as they passed. "Just put your gifts on the account, as usual," he instructed Penelope.

"Thank you. I'll see you at home." She placed a kiss on his weathered cheek and wandered over to the silver selection, poking through the tea sets and fine picture frames.

She perused furnishings, glassware, small portraits, and baby-related goods. Tucked away in the corner was a lovely little table clock that sported two gilded bulls supporting the clock's delicate face. Penelope remembered how Charlotte had said the bull was featured on the MacLeod family crest and promptly called a shop girl over.

"Pardon me, but I'd like to have that clock wrapped as a wedding gift," Penelope said to the young girl.

"Yes, Miss Elmsly." The shop girl bobbed a

small curtsey and hurried away with Penelope's purchase.

Penelope meandered over to the registers where a cashier had already brought out the Elmsly purchase book, which recorded everything the family bought from the arcade. She swiftly signed her name, pleased to see that the elegant clock was very reasonably priced.

"Is there anything else I can get for you, Miss Elmsly?" the shop girl asked as she presented Penelope with a box wrapped carefully in pale blue paper.

"Yes." She frowned at the plain box, thinking it rather bare. "Please fetch me some hat bobbles for the box. I'm thinking some of those silk orange blossoms and a white ribbon to dress it up a little."

The girl returned promptly with the requested items, as well as a pair of ivory-handled scissors. Penelope arranged the simulated flowers around the newly ribbon-tied box, pleased with how festive her gift looked. She thanked the shop girl for her help and left the arcade, nodding in thanks to her carriage driver as he helped her up to her seat.

She rode with the gift held firmly on her lap, watching the people strolling along the walking paths and other carriages as they passed. Some had crests on their doors and Penelope was familiar with each. Holly leaves encircled a lion for the Beaucannons, three crescent moons below a pair of swords belonged to the Drake family, a rather disgruntled looking bull—

"Stop the carriage!" she called out, a wide grin breaking out on her lips.

"Change of plans, miss?" the driver asked from his perch as he heaved in the reins.

"Take me to the MacLeod house. Do you know it?"

"Yes, Miss." He urged the horses forward.

***

The Elmsly carriage pulled up right behind the MacLeod carriage, and Penelope hopped out without even waiting for assistance. She could see Conner helping Charlotte climb out in a flurry of plaid and ruffles.

"Charlotte!" Penelope exclaimed, her present for them tucked in her arms.

Charlotte turned at the sound of her name and smiled widely as she saw her oldest friend hurrying to meet her. "Oh, Penelope, I'm *so* happy to see you!"

Penelope pulled her into a one-armed hug. "I can't believe you're here! I've only just received your letter."

"Oh, yes, we're quite on our own in the Highlands, so it takes ever so long for our mail to reach its destination." Charlotte pulled back. "I have so much to tell you!"

"All good things, I hope." Penelope turned to Conner, who was looking splendid in his traditional kilted garb. "Conner, you are well?"

"Aye, married life suits me verra fine." He grinned, shooting a pointed look at Charlotte, who instantly pinked.

Penelope frowned. "Married life? But your note

said you were to be married *here*?"

"It's such a long story." Charlotte sighed. "But a very good one. Come in from the cold and I'll call for tea. I'm positively famished."

"Aye, go on," Conner said. "I'm goin' to wait here for the wagons with our things."

Charlotte and Penelope entered the MacLeod townhome together, greeted by a pair of maids who instantly began fussing over their cloaks and promising tea and sandwiches. Another maid led them to a cozy sitting room where Penelope and Charlotte both took seats upon a beautifully upholstered settee.

"So strange, I've only been in this room in passing and now it seems it is *my* sitting room," Charlotte mused, looking around.

"That must feel odd."

"Yes, I feel much more at home in the castle."

"Oh, but of course," Penelope said, her voice edged with good-natured sarcasm. It was very much like Charlotte to sound so blasé about living in a castle like a princess in a fairytale.

Charlotte giggled. "Do stop teasing. You know I just like the country more. Always have."

"Before I forget, this is for you." She held out the gift. "I was actually on my way home when I saw your carriage. It's a wedding present."

"It's so pretty, I almost don't want to open it!" Charlotte said as she carefully removed the silk blossoms and ribbon. When the clock was finally revealed, she gasped. "Penelope, it's gorgeous. I love it."

"Now that we've gotten this out of the way, I'm

dying to hear what's going on! A *marriage*? Why wasn't I invited? And what's become of Richard Howard? He never came back to London and my father hasn't heard anything of him in quite some time."

"That's because he is never coming back," she said firmly, her fingers tracing one bull's legs.

"You mean he is to stay on in Scotland?"

Charlotte placed the clock carefully on the mantle above the fireplace and sat beside Penelope, pausing before beginning her tale. "I believe I need to tell you the whole story in order to answer that, but I hardly know where to start. Well, I've found out that Conner has no illegitimate children."

"That's always good to know."

"He merely helped his sister's friend find a home for her son and the gossipers ran with it. After that was revealed, we really got to know each other and fell in love. Then vile Richard Howard came to try and bring me back to England with a band of hired men."

"Yes, so your note said, but please tell me more!" Penelope's heart fluttered at the thrilling tale. It had been so long since she had any excitement outside of new hats or a particularly tasty crumpet.

"Yes. But Conner sent him away and we thought we heard the last of it. After that is when Conner asked for my permission to officially court me. Once we entered into that stage of our relationship, one of the kitchen maids got extremely jealous. She poisoned my tea for days before Conner found out that someone was trying to kill me."

"Goodness, what a turn of events. I hope she was punished severely!"

Charlotte grimaced. "I'm getting to that. Well, I felt rather sorry for the maid—Nettie was her name—and I helped her leave the castle."

"Why in the world would you do such a silly thing, letting a murderess roam the countryside like that?"

"I thought she was not all there, in the head, I mean. And I made her promise to not come back."

Penelope raised an elegant eyebrow. "Certainly you're joking?"

She averted her eyes and picked at something upon her spotless skirt. "It was a very grave mistake. She joined forces with Richard to kidnap me so he could have me as his bride and she could win Conner. Not that it would have worked, of course."

"Of course," Penelope agreed with a firm nod.

"Well, Nettie showed Richard a secret tunnel that allowed him to steal me from the castle and spirit me away to a church where a cruel priest was gong to marry me against my will. My father and Abigail were there."

Heat rose up her cheeks and along her neck as she thought of the duke going along with such an evil scheme. "And they were privy to this terrible plan?"

"No! Neither had any idea. In fact, Abigail helped me escape England in the first place, so she certainly wasn't going to knowingly go along with Richard."

"Did she?" Penelope was confused. Abigail had

never struck her as someone who would help a young lady run away in the dead of night. Let alone her own stepdaughter.

Charlotte nodded. "Yes. She gave me some money and bid me a safe journey."

"What a little minx."

"But, as I was saying, Richard had tricked my father and once he saw what a brute Richard was, he tried to help, but he had hired violent men. Thankfully, Conner arrived and saved me."

"Good old Conner!" Penelope liked him even more now, if that were possible. "But what happened to Richard Howard?"

"Conner killed him," Charlotte answered in a quiet tone. "He was buried outside the church grounds. I don't know what happened afterward, as Conner didn't want me to feel any guilt."

"Is he truly dead? There was talk that something had to have happened to him during his travels, but no one knew for certain."

"It was the only way he would have ever let us be. Looking back, I think he would have killed me before letting Conner have me, if it came to that."

Penelope nodded slowly, the idea of murder, no matter how virtuous, still making her stomach turn. "Then I suppose Conner did the right the right thing."

Charlotte grimaced. "Perhaps. I'm just glad it's over now. And on a brighter note, my father begged my forgiveness and now Conner and I are to be properly married."

"He said you were already married."

"It's complicated." Charlotte paused as a maid

entered carrying a silver tray with tea and snacks and left it for the women to serve themselves. She immediately piled her plate high with cakes as Penelope selected a cucumber sandwich for herself. "You see, Scotland has a tradition called hand fasting, in which a man and woman can live together as a married couple for a year and a day. They must be married when that time comes to a close, or go their separate ways."

"How very queer," Penelope said as she took a sip of tea. "So are you married, or no?"

"Technically, yes. We said our vows before witnesses, but we must be married in a church for it to be lasting."

"Ah, I see. What a jolly custom!"

"It's rather nice to be married to Conner. He's a good husband."

"In more ways than one, I presume?" Penelope shot her a mischievous grin.

Charlotte blushed. "Goodness, Penelope, you're terrible!"

She laughed, happy to finally be able to jest with a dear friend. "Oh, tell me something I don't know!"

"Now, tell me what's new with you," Charlotte pleaded through a mouthful of cake.

"Nothing on the same page as your happenings. No one's tried to murder me and I haven't been kidnapped. All in all, it's been rather dull."

"True, but you must have been up to some kind of trouble while I've been away?"

Penelope poked at her sandwich. "Hardly. It's been quite boring without you. I've had to go to all the rest of the season's balls and talk to the likes of Greta Hallstone all evening instead of having a good gossip with you over punch."

"No special man?"

Penelope took off her new hat. The pins were poking into her scalp. "Nothing on the horizon either. I thought that Thomas Land might be a good match but my father and his father don't get along for some reason. So, that was out of the question."

"I would have thought your parents would have arranged a marriage by now."

"No, their marriage was a love match, so they want the same for me. But they never think anyone is up for the task. By the time someone does come along, I'll be positively geriatric."

"What's the plan, then?"

"Besides dying old and alone with a posse of ill-behaved poodles to leave my fortune to? Well, my parents are putting together a ball for my birthday, after wedding season is over. They hope that by then all the eligible men who haven't been snapped up will be a little more willing to propose."

"How romantic," Charlotte teased.

"Perhaps I'll find my own Scottish king to run off with. It seems to have worked out rather well for you."

"Well, what *do* you want?"

"I honestly don't know anymore. I used to think that I'd be swept off my feet by a lovely duke who adored me, owned homes in both the country and city, and would have a few children by now. But, I'm two seasons out without a husband in sight."

"You're only twenty."

"Yes, but soon I'll be twenty-*one*. My parents are pushing for marriage, but chase off any serious suitors. I've almost lost hope that I'll ever be allowed to marry. At this point, I suppose I'd accept anyone decent who came my way."

"I'm sure you'll find someone this year." Charlotte placed a hand upon Penelope's. "And he'll be tall, dashing, a wonderful dancer, and offer you everything you've ever dreamed."

"I do hope so, Charlotte. But enough about my dreaded spinsterhood, let's talk floral arrangements and tablecloths for your grand affair!"

Charlotte rolled her eyes. "Let's not."

"You can't deny me the pleasure of planning your wedding, can you?" She pouted dramatically. "Who else do you know who can plan a gala event in a week's time?"

"No one."

"Then do stop moping and cheer up. We have a wedding to discuss!"

Chapter Two

"Charlotte, you look so lovely." Penelope adjusted the delicate lace veil that flowed over her friend's slim shoulders. They had played 'bride' in their youth with Penelope dressing up in her mother's gowns and forcing a bored Charlotte to be the groom. But, now they weren't playing pretend.

"I can scarcely believe it." Penelope let out an excited giggled. "You were once so opposed to marriage and now you're possibly ready to run down the aisle!"

"It feels rather different when you're marrying for love. Conner's everything I could have hoped for in a husband."

She felt a pang of sadness, but tried to swallow it quickly like a bitter tonic. While she loved that her best friend had found a true soul mate, Penelope couldn't help but feel a rather strange sensation of unadulterated jealousy. "I do hope I can find a great love like that," she admitted in a whisper.

"Perhaps next season. You've already denied so many men." Charlotte smiled.

She tapped her chin with a gloved hand. "Well, since Conner doesn't have a brother, I suppose I'll have to keep looking in London for someone who worships me like he does you."

Charlotte laughed, squeezing Penelope's hand. "You will visit me, yes?"

"As often as I can." And Penelope meant it; she longed to see the rolling hills and gray seas that Charlotte had described. "Although, I do suppose you'll come back quite frequently to oversee the running of your children's home."

"Of course. I'll be visiting after my honeymoon to christen the opening of my orphanage."

"And then you can tell me all about your wedding night and your wonderful time in Paris!"

"My *second* wedding night."

Penelope poked Charlotte in the arm. "You're blushing!"

"Well, I should be blushing. I'm a bride."

She glanced at the clock, noting that it was almost time for the ceremony to begin. "We really must go. Your father's waiting to walk you down the aisle and we're almost late."

"Do I look all right?"

Penelope took in Charlotte's angelic gown. With all its pickups, fine bows, and carefully placed lace, she looked divine. "Like a positively delicious confection!"

The girls walked arm in arm up to the front doors of the Holloway family cathedral. Penelope herself had decorated the entryway with strands of ivy leaves and sprigs of orange blossoms earlier that morning. She had put as many green, living things into the church as possible in order to make it feel a bit more Scottish.

"I'll go in now," Penelope whispered as she passed Charlotte her bouquet.

She slipped quietly through the doors and walked down to the front of the chapel and sat on the end of the first row next to Charlotte's stepmother, Abigail. Abigail had always been fond of Penelope, believing her to be the ideal young woman; poised, delicate, polite, and not one to run off into fields barefoot and jump in a lake, one of Charlotte's favorite pastimes. Now the woman was positively beside herself with emotion, gripping Penelope's hand tightly and crying about how happy Conner and Charlotte would be together. How times had changed.

Penelope glanced up at the altar toward Conner, who looked very regal in his usual kilt. However, he had taken his dress a bit further and added a very savage looking sword, a dress coat, and a jaunty little cap with several feathers on it. He winked at her as their eyes met, making Penelope even more glad that he would be marrying Charlotte. She deserved a jolly man like Conner.

When the doors finally opened, the organist struck up the traditional wedding march. The guests all stood to watch Charlotte and her father walk down the aisle. Penelope was beginning to lose feeling in the hand Abigail held, but wouldn't pull away. As she scanned the crowd to see their awed expressions, her eyes met another's.

A pair of brilliant green orbs gazed at her from a tanned, rugged face framed by wavy brown hair. He had a sculpted jaw and a set of full lips that were set in a steady line. The man himself stood taller than anyone else in the crowd with broad shoulders and massive arms that Penelope could see the outlines of through his coat. He also wore a kilt, but one that wasn't in the MacLeod yellows, but one of blood reds and blacks. It made him look almost savage.

His stare was one that she found both unsettling and strangely enticing. He looked as if he knew something she did not, and longed to tell her the secret. Penelope tried to tear her gaze away, but stayed captivated by the man. He had the look of dashing danger that she had read about in novels. He even seemed more…*Scottish* than Conner, who was the only Scot she really knew familiarly. She could picture this new mysterious man on horseback, maybe holding a sword.

Penelope looked away as Charlotte passed her pew, her cheeks burning. No one had ever stared that intently at her before. It was as if she was naked before him and he could peer into her very soul.

She brushed the feelings aside and focused on her friends' wedding vows. But she could still feel the green eyes upon her. Small shivers, like an electrical current, ran up her limbs and settled deep in her chest, leaving her with an uncomfortable hum of awareness.

***

"Charlotte, that was a wonderful ceremony, even with the bit where Conner snorted and called out the priest for the vows!" Penelope gently hugged her friend, careful not to muss her wedding gown. "I have never been to a more beautiful and ridiculously amusing wedding."

They sat together in the Holloway ballroom where the wedding breakfast was being held. Penelope sat to Charlotte's left with Conner's sisters Flora and Gwen on her other side. Seated next to Charlotte was her new husband followed by a gentle giant called Big Angus, and Ian, the little orphan boy Conner had taken to ward. The mysterious green-eyed man was there, too, and now poked curiously at the goat cheese tart upon his plate. Penelope and Charlotte savored their few moments together as both knew Charlotte would soon be gone to Paris for her honeymoon.

"I still can't believe I managed to find a husband," Charlotte whispered. "I was honestly quite sure that I'd die an old spinster and be extremely happy about it."

"But now you get to die a queen, which I believe to be much more fun. Why, I wish *I* could find an excuse to traipse around my castle with a crown on, you lucky cow," Penelope joked, scrunching her nose prettily. "Say, Char, I know Big Angus and Ian, but who is that man at the end?"

Charlotte looked down Conner's side of the table as if she'd forgotten who was there. "Oh, you haven't met? That's one of Conner's Scottish cousins, Drummond MacGregor."

"Drummond MacGregor." She felt a tingle upon her lips as she said his name.

Charlotte narrowed her eyes. "I know that look."

Penelope snapped to attention and stabbed a

piece of lamb with her fork. "What look?"

"You get the same look on your face when your father's shop gets a shipment of new hats. Penelope, I don't see any hats at my bridal table."

"I was just admiring the décor."

"I wasn't aware the décor included a Scotsman named Drummond."

Penelope bit her lip. "Don't talk about things you don't know. I truly was just looking at the lovely floral displays."

Charlotte snorted. "You act like I don't know you. I'm quite sure you were looking at Drummond."

Penelope daintily took a bite of her lamb, chewing slowly, as to buy herself more time. "Char," she began, "I am just trying to learn the names of all your Scottish guests. He happened to be the closest stranger."

"Well, then, I must introduce you so you won't be strangers anymore!"

Penelope paled, knowing what her friend was about to do. "Don't."

Charlotte lowered her voice. "Do you remember how at the New Year's Eve ball I was hiding from Conner and you called him over even when I begged you not to?"

"Oh, please, don't."

"I'm sorry, but I must." Charlotte turned away and leaned over the table, gazing toward the far end. "Oh, Drummond?"

Drummond MacGregor looked up. "My lady?"

"Have you met my dearest friend, Penelope Elmsly?" Charlotte motioned to Penelope with an ungloved hand.

"No, my lady. I have no' had the pleasure."

"Well, then, Drummond MacGregor, meet Penelope Elmsly." She introduced them in the most impolite manner, but none of the Scots at the table seemed to notice. And Conner, who was watching his wife, looked over at Penelope with a smirk on his lips.

Drummond nodded. "A pleasure to make your acquaintance."

"Likewise." Penelope tried to keep her voice even, but found it faltered and she turned her attention to her spiced wine, taking a rather unladylike gulp.

"See? No longer strangers." Charlotte giggled. "Oh, I've been waiting months to get you back for that."

"That was terribly rude, yelling over the table like that," Penelope chastised with a gentle wag of a finger. "If you wanted us to meet then you should have made proper introductions that didn't include sticking your elbow in a tart."

Charlotte took her napkin and cleaned the worst of the cheese and berry filling off her arm. "Scotland isn't like England. Yes, there are rules, but not like here. In Scotland, the dinners are loud and warm with all the men in attendance. There's singing and jokes, not perfectly quiet dining where you're served every dish by a butler in livery."

"I don't see the allure."

"That's because you're a fully proper lady while I am only—"

"The parts of a lady that counts." Penelope

grinned, alluding to her womanly charms.

"Well, there's the Penelope I know," she mumbled, her lips curled into a smirk.

Penelope pushed away her plate. "Is it almost time for some dancing? It's been a good week without a nice spin around a ballroom."

"I'm not sure. My father seems content to just eat for hours." Charlotte placed a hand on her husband's arm. "Conner, do you think you can go tell the musicians that we'd like to dance now?"

Conner patted Charlotte's hands and rose from the table, heading toward the band.

"I'm glad he isn't a womanizing cad after all," Penelope mused as Conner blended into the crowd. "I can't imagine you marrying anyone else."

"Me either," Charlotte said dreamily.

Conner was back in an instant as the band began playing, holding out a hand. "A dance, wife?"

"Of course, husband." Charlotte allowed herself to be led away onto the dance floor. Soon, several other couples followed them into a jaunty number.

"May I?" Little Ian had hopped from his seat to ask Penelope to dance. His small face was so eager and he was positively adorable in his tiny kilt and jacket. He looked every bit the miniature Scottish laird.

"Certainly, sir," she answered seriously. "Thank you for this honor."

Penelope and Ian held hands and shuffled together in the most improper manner. He tried to copy the other dancer's steps, stumbling over his own feet in an attempt to keep up. Penelope tried to suppress a giggle as he complimented her on her graceful movements.

"Might I cut in, lad?" a man asked.

Pausing, Penelope looked up to see Drummond MacGregor standing there, his expression placid and unaffected by the excitement around him. "Oh, hello," she said.

"Well, I suppose so," Ian replied, eyeing the maids who were clearing a table to bring out the cake. "I have important business, ye see?"

"Aye, lad. Ye go about your business and I'll see to the lady," MacGregor said as Ian scampered away to sneak into the kitchen. "Care to dance, Miss Elmsly?" he asked her. His voice was deep and echoed in her chest, sucking all the air from her lungs.

"Y-yes, of course." She cleared her throat and placed her left hand on his shoulder and her right hand in his.

As they entered into the throng of dancers, Penelope found herself marveling at how positively massive MacGregor was. His hand seemed to fully encompass her own silk-covered one. She would have to strain her neck to look at him, but found that she couldn't bring herself to do it, although she subconsciously knew that his eyes were fixed on her. Penelope could feel his hot gaze boring into her, seeking, searching—for what she did not know.

But for his size he wasn't a terribly clumsy dancer, as most large men were. He seemed to have a gentle quietness in him that she was sure came in handy while he participated in all sorts of manly pursuits such as hunting, tracking, rock throwing, whatever it was Scottish men did when they weren't horseback riding shirtless over green hills.

MacGregor slowed and peered down at her in concern. "Ye seem to be verra flushed, Miss Elmsly."

It was true. Penelope felt her face heat, warmed by the thought of him doing rugged Scottish things. The entire idea was ridiculously unladylike. "Oh, I'm fine. It's just a tad warm in here."

He slowed them to a stop at the edge of the dance floor. "Aye, it is. Shall I fetch ye a drink, then?"

"That would be lovely, thank you," Penelope said as she opened her fan.

She watched him enter the crowd, parting it as he was Moses and the wedding guests were the red sea. Even at a distance, she could see the back of his head, higher than the rest. Penelope turned her attention back to the dancers, fanning herself all the while. She couldn't understand what peculiar feeling MacGregor stirred within her. Of course, he was an attractive man, if one cared to fancy rough outdoorsman with long hair, immense shoulders, and a graceful confidence that came from a life of diligent hard work. Penelope certainly didn't, or at least that's what she told herself.

"Dear me." Penelope sighed, her fan fluttering faster.

"Your drink," MacGregor said above her, holding out a decanter of punch.

"Thank you, Mister MacGregor," she said, taking the glass. As she did, her fingers brushed his, zapping her with a delicious shock of electricity.

"Fine weddin'," he stated evenly, scanning the

crowd.

Penelope nodded. "Oh, yes. Everything is quite lovely. It will be the talk of things for quite some time."

"Ye are an old friend o' Lady Charlotte?"

"Yes, we've been best friends since we were very small. I'll miss her terribly when she's in Scotland."

"Do no' fash. The MacLeod says he plans on spendin' a good deal o' time here."

"I thought Conner was your cousin. Why do you still call him the MacLeod?" Penelope knew her line of questioning was a bit too intimate, but she found herself even more curious about the colossal Scot as she observed him.

"He might be my kin, but he is also my chieftain," MacGregor explained, his arms crossed over his muscular chest. "It would be a great disservice to forget who I fight for, when in public."

"What other pastimes do you employ in Scotland, Mister MacGregor?"

"Nothin' much that ye'd find interestin', just a wee bit o' archery and whatever tasks the MacLeod needs a hand with."

"Oh, how terribly noble," Penelope mumbled into her cup. MacGregor might be a fine dish of a man, but she began to believe he might be little more than a handsome face. The man's life seemed to almost completely revolve around Conner. She had never been a fan of anyone who took things too seriously.

Charlotte popped up next to Penelope. "Has anyone seen Conner?"

"Lost your husband already?" Penelope laughed.

"Shall I find him for ye, Lady Charlotte?" MacGregor asked.

"I suppose so. Thank you, Drummond." Charlotte took Penelope's half-empty glass of punch.

"My lady." He bowed slightly.

After MacGregor had left in search of his lord, Charlotte turned to Penelope eagerly. "So? Are you mad for him yet? Have you caught the Scottish fever?"

Penelope grimaced. "The Scottish fever? You're beginning to sound like me. And, no, he's not quite my type."

"Why ever not?" Charlotte drank her stolen punch.

"He's devilishly good-looking, but he seems a tad too uptight and boring for my tastes."

"Boring? Hardly! He's the most accomplished archer, can play the bagpipes wonderfully, and always bags the first stag of the hunt."

Penelope stared at her blankly. "So?"

"So, he's *not* boring. I thought you two would get along famously." Charlotte huffed, her mouth turning downward.

The events on the day clicked and Penelope gasped. "Were you trying to set us up?"

She shrugged. "Well, you had said you wished Conner had a brother. I thought a cousin might be the next best thing, and Drum's the most eye-catching and benevolent of them all."

"You thought wrongly," Penelope scolded. "Do you remember what I said I wanted in a husband?"

Charlotte paused. "All I really recall is that you wanted someone to cherish you and that you liked being a china doll, or something of the sort."

"Exactly." She closed her fan with a snap. "You hate corsets and hats and balls and arranging flowers for perfectly executed dinner parties. I, however, value the importance of societal rules and regulations."

"But you're the one who told me to cause a scandal with Conner on New Year's Eve. You didn't see the importance of rules then."

"You aren't made for following the rules. I am. That is why you're marvelous at being a Scottish queen. Your love of horses and the outdoors, and leaving your hair unpinned, is very much who you are and it's very much accepted there. Could you imagine me taking a Scottish husband and riding a horse bareback with my hair down, corset entirely forgotten?"

"I suppose you're right." Charlotte frowned at her empty decanter. "It was just wishful thinking that you and Drummond would fall madly in love and then you could come live with me in Scotland."

Penelope felt a pang in her heart upon thinking about her departure. "Oh, Char, we'll see each other plenty! And, now that you're not on the run, you can write me twice a week. Three times, if something worth noting happens."

"There's my wife!" Conner appeared, trailed by MacGregor. Conner had disposed of his jacket somewhere and brushed Charlotte's cheek with a knuckle. "Are ye well?"

"Well enough, now that you've been returned to

me," Charlotte answered sweetly.

Penelope snickered at her friend's sudden relapse into a soft tone that she obviously only used with Conner. "You two are almost too much."

"Just wait," Conner said. "Soon enough ye'll be simperin' up to your own man."

"That reminds me," Charlotte started, "Penelope is having a birthday ball next month. Will we be back in early July?"

He rubbed his chin. "Aye, we can be. Three weeks is enough time to spend in Paris."

"Oh, you must come!" Penelope pleaded. "You both are just so much fun at parties. And, Conner, all of your family and, er, *men* are invited. You'll receive a formal invitation shortly, but I'll be ever so pleased to cross you all off my list."

"On that note, Penelope, my sister Flora will be stayin' on in London for a spell," Conner said. "Would ye mind checkin' in on her when ye can? She has no' much experience with London society and I'd like her to have a friend here."

"Conner wants her away from a man she fancies," Charlotte elaborated, much to his obvious annoyance.

"Oh? Is he a bad match?"

"No, he seems quite nice. Conner just thinks that Jasper is too old and hard for Flora and she isn't cut out for life as a farmer's wife."

"A farmer's wife?" Although Penelope didn't know Flora well at all, she couldn't imagine the slight Scottish girl planting potatoes in one of the fine silk gowns she wore. "Oh, I see, you're hoping to find her a good match in England? I know a few eligible men if you'd like me to make introductions."

Conner pursed his lips. "I'll no' say that. I just thought a bit o' distance would make her see he was just a passin' fancy. He's no good for her."

Penelope raised an eyebrow. "Oh, what a coincidence. That's what I thought of you and Charlotte. Yet, here we are!"

Charlotte laughed openly. "Do you still want Penelope looking after Flora?"

He shook his head. "Well, now I'm no' so sure."

"All jokes aside, I can promise she won't be running off to elope, or any other such nonsense," Penelope said. "If it's one thing I'm a great believer in, it's the importance of a proper wedding and immaculately planned ball afterward."

"How comfortin'," Conner said wryly. "But, I do appreciate ye lookin' out for her."

"Just promise to come to my birthday and I'll be sure to see to it that she's cared for." Penelope smiled in a way she hoped was charming.

Conner nodded and turned to his wife. "It's almost time to go."

"Oh!" Charlotte held up her bouquet. "I suppose I must dispose of this so we might make our escape. Goodbye, Penelope. I'll write you as soon as I'm settled."

She wrapped her arms around Charlotte, tears pooling in her eyes. "I'll miss you terribly."

"I'll be back before you know it." Charlotte gave her a final squeeze before letting go.

Conner took her hand and led her halfway up the ballroom's staircase, then clapped his hands loudly to garner attention. “Thank ye all for comin’ to share with us the beginnin’ o’ our married life. Now we’ll be off to our honeymoon. But first, Charlotte would like to toss her bouquet!”

Penelope stepped back into the crowd as the other unmarried ladies crowded below Charlotte, their hands held high in anticipation. She wasn’t all that interested in highlighting her unmarried status. Besides, she had already heard a bit of tittering about how her younger, wilder, friend had managed to land a husband before her and couldn’t bear to add more fuel to the fire.

“Penelope, do stop hiding!” Charlotte called out jovially. “Join the fun!”

Pinking, Penelope reluctantly stepped forward to the group of women, staying on the edge of the pack. But when Charlotte pitched the bundle of orange blossoms to the floor, they smacked Penelope in the chest, leaving her holding the prized bouquet.

“You little minx,” Penelope breathed, glaring up at Charlotte.

Charlotte blew her a kiss before taking off up the rest of the stairs with Conner.

Flora came up to Penelope, the MacLeod grin upon her lips. “I believe my dear sister did that on purpose.

“And I believe you’re right,” Penelope agreed, holding out the flowers. “Do you want them?”

Flora shook her head. “It’s bad luck to give the whole bouquet away. If you do, and I accept, then both of us are doomed to spinsterhood and I believe we’re much too fine a catch to have that happen.”

"Lovely," she muttered, her mind drifting to thoughts of her own impending unmarried future.

"But I will take one *little* bloom, for luck." Flora plucked one of the small white flowers and slipped it into her braided hair. She then saw Gwen in the crowed and dashed off, promising to see Penelope again soon.

Even though Charlotte and Conner had left for their trip, the ball went on, and would for many hours. Penelope could see Charlotte's father, the Duke of Glenwood, mixing with the crowd, his face red with drink. Not wishing to partake in the party without her friend, she slipped back to her table and took a seat, noticing Ian's feet sticking out from under the linen.

Penelope lifted the tablecloth and peered inside. Ian's face was covered in icing. "Enjoying the wedding?"

"Aye." Ian held up a half eaten piece of cake. "Cook said I could have as much as I wanted."

"That's nice. Would you like to sit at the table like a little gentleman?"

Ian's little face scrunched up in thought for a moment before he shook his head. "No, thank you. I like my hideaway."

Penelope nodded in understanding. "If I were small enough, I'd join you. But I'll leave you to it, instead." She dropped the tablecloth and sat back in her chair, fingering the orange blossoms in her lap. While Flora promised the bouquet was good luck, Penelope had very little faith that the tiny flowers would be enough to get her married.

Although, from across the ballroom, she could

see a pair of vivid green eyes watching her intently. While they held her gaze for a moment, Penelope could only stare for so long before she had to look away.

Chapter Three

"None of these are any good." Penelope's mother sighed as she pushed the pile of invitations and letters away from her with distaste.

Penelope took the cards and flipped through them. "There can't be something wrong with all of these men? Surely there's one you don't hate."

"Well, there is," she said, patting her bun. "Wently is a known gambler. And this Parker's just only lost his wife in the childbed a few weeks ago, completely shameful for him to try to call when he should be mourning. And Teeson—don't get me started on Teeson!"

"And what did he do that is so offensive? Murder? Rob a bank? Wear a black morning coat to tea when the occasion *obviously* called for a gray one?"

Cecily narrowed her eyes. "He is often late paying his dues to your father's arcade. Not because he doesn't have the funds, but because he is merely lazy. Although I wouldn't put it past him to wear the wrong jacket."

"That cad."

"Don't jest, Penelope. It makes you look common."

"So, none of these men are up to snuff. Shall we begin to import some from other countries, perhaps?"

Cecily paused, her eyes wide. "Now there's an idea."

"Goodness, Mother, I was joking!" Penelope stood from the breakfast table. "At the rate you're dismissing men, I'll never be married and it will be all your fault, and Father's."

"Now, Penelope—"

"Please don't 'now, Penelope' me. I've gone two seasons without a husband because you chase off any eligible men. If you want me to be a spinster and stay at home with you in your advanced age, then I would appreciate some honesty."

"That's not the case at all!" Her face fell into a mixture of confusion and sympathy. "We just want the best for you."

"Then stop pushing everyone away. If you want to help, let me find a match and stay out of it!" She turned from the table and headed toward the main hall.

"Penelope, where are you going?"

"I'm going to go see Flora. At least she knows something about rejected suitors." Penelope grabbed her cloak from a maid and left the house, not bothering to call for a carriage.

The walk to the MacLeod home was long enough to help clear her head. While she knew, or thought she knew, that her parents kept her close out of love, she still had difficulty understanding their motivations. For years, all her parents spoke of was how she would find a husband, have children, and live a life outside the Elmsly home. But now, it looked as if they intended the complete opposite. While Penelope was against running off with a suitor, she was beginning to see the allure.

"Good morning, Miss Elmsly," a maid greeted her at the door, taking her cape.

"Is Flora at home?" Penelope asked.

"Yes, Miss Elmsly. She's in the library." She led her down the main hall and through another corridor before depositing her at the door.

When Penelope entered the library, she smiled, recalling that it was the place where Conner and Penelope shared a torrid embrace. "So, this is the scene of the crime?"

"That is it," Flora said from her perch upon an armchair. She had seemingly read her mind. "It's so nice to see you, Penelope. I've been going quite mad these three days since the wedding. I haven't been out at all."

"No? Well, that won't do. Shall we go out, then?"

Flora perked up. "And do what?"

"Anything you like. We can go for a walk in the park, have some tea at the Stoneward Hotel, or go to the shops."

"We must go shopping. In Scotland we only have whatever the merchants bring to choose from. By the time it comes to us, it's positively picked over."

Penelope clapped her hands. "Splendid! I do love

to go shopping! We can go to my father's arcade."

"Arcade? What's that?"

"It's a rather new invention. Inside one large building are all sorts of goods for purchase—dresses, hats, paintings, fans, all under one roof."

"What an interesting idea. I've never heard of such a thing." Flora stood, motioning for Penelope to follow her. "I'll call for a carriage, and our cloaks, and we'll be off at once."

When they came to the great hall, a lad having been sent to fetch the carriage, the girls slipped on their capes and touched up their hair in the reflection of the mirror-lined walls. Penelope didn't think to put on a hat before she left home, instead leaving in just a pale purple gown and sable cloak. She felt rather naked without one. At least her hair was suitably pinned up.

"I must get a hat while we're out. If we go out to tea, I can't look a fright."

Flora laughed. "Must I get one too, then? We often don't wear hats in Scotland, outside of when it rains."

Penelope studied Flora, a lovely waif in a sea-foam silk dress. Her dark blonde hair fell down her shoulders in waves. "I don't believe so. You look like a fairy queen. I almost want to put a crown of flowers upon your head and release you into the forest."

"Such flattery." She sounded pleased.

The front door opened and Drummond MacGregor entered, bowing slightly at them both. "The carriage is ready."

"Oh, Drum is coming with us," Flora said,

leading the way outside. "Conner says I'm not to go anywhere without him."

"A bodyguard," Penelope whispered. What a bodyguard MacGregor made. With his massive size and constant vigilance, Conner couldn't have found a more menacing watchdog for his sister. No one would dare look at her from the other side of the road, let alone actually speak to her.

MacGregor helped both ladies into the carriage and then took his place on the back step—an impromptu footman.

"He could have sat in the carriage with us," Penelope said.

Flora shook her head as the carriage began the short journey to The Piccadilly Emporium. "No, he can't. The ceiling is too low, so it's rather uncomfortable for him."

"Understandable, I suppose." Penelope watched out the window.

When they got to the arcade, MacGregor helped both of them onto the road, following at a short distance as they entered the building. Penelope saw the heads of the shoppers turn as MacGregor passed. She also noticed more than one look from an appreciative lady, which turned her stomach in a rather peculiar way.

"Good morning, Miss Elmsly." A shop girl approached them. "Would you or your guests require any assistance this morning?"

"No, thank you. This is Lady MacLeod and her cousin Mister MacGregor. I'll call for you if your assistance is required."

"How fancy." Flora sounded impressed as she

wandered over to a far wall where some of the newest novels were on display in neat rows upon a wide shelf.

"Just like a MacLeod to go right to the books!" Penelope laughed, turning to MacGregor. "Do you read much?"

MacGregor shifted slightly before answering. "No' much, Miss Elmsly."

She flapped a hand. "Oh, do stop calling me Miss Elmsly. You're cousins with Conner who is married to my greatest friend, whom is like a sister to me, making us almost…half cousins by marriage, perhaps? Nonetheless, call me Penelope, please."

"Aye." He nodded and began scanning the room again for assassins, or perhaps a nicely sized buck. Either way, Penelope wished he would lighten up a bit. Nothing was going to happen in her father's establishment.

"Flora, have you found anything?" Penelope asked.

She held up a pile of freshly bound books. "I feel as if I should get them all, just in case."

"I thought Conner always brought the newest novels back to Scotland with him?" Penelope picked up an illustrated book of fairytales and flipped open the cover.

"He does, but they're usually military books, or something history-based," Flora explained. "They're nice and all, but sometimes I'd just like to curl up before the fire with a good mystery or romance."

"Completely understandable," Penelope decided, beckoning a sales girl to begin piles for them as they shopped. "Just hand in your things and we'll sign our ledgers at the front when we're ready."

"How terribly modern." Flora gladly handed over her stack. "Didn't you say you wanted a hat?"

The women kept shopping, perusing the fanciful goods with MacGregor hot on their heels, occasionally reaching up to fetch something on a high shelf or staring someone down who had their hands on a last coveted pair of gloves. Penelope thought MacGregor was a nice addition to their little shopping party, even if he was a man of extremely few words.

"I'm famished," Penelope said as their items were boxed up for them. She pinned a new hat upon her piled curls as she spoke. She was proud of her most recent addition—a wide-brimmed, white confection with a cheerful lilac bow that matched her gown perfectly. "Shall we take tea at Stoneward? My treat."

"That would be delightful." Flora signed her name to her new account at The Piccadilly Emporium. "Drum, you don't have any other pressing plans, do you?"

"No. I go where ye go." His voice was even, as always, but when he said those words, his gaze strayed to Penelope, seeming to take on a warmer shade of green.

"Right, then." Penelope cleared her throat, leading the way out of the store, followed by Flora, then MacGregor, and bringing up the rear were three boys carrying their paper wrapped packages to be loaded into the carriage.

"Tight fit." Flora giggled, the seat next to her

piled with their purchases.

"Necessities, really. You needed a good parasol in case you decide to go walking in the park. And gloves are always a must. You also need a hat for every day of the week, and multiple ones for Sunday—one for church and one for visiting after church."

"And, to think, my brother once thought that *I* was high maintenance." Flora touched the gray hat Penelope had fastened to her hastily pinned up hair. "A hat for every day of the week."

"Your brother will hardly recognize you when he comes back from his honeymoon. And neither will your man back in Scotland."

Flora flushed prettily. "Don't tease. He's not really *my* man, anyway."

"Well, your temporary man, then. No one says you have to marry him. While a honey tongued man may be fine for a dance, he will never make as good a husband as his quiet companion," Penelope stated knowingly. She then lowered her voice. "The quiet ones are always the easiest to mold."

"Mold?"

"Yes, mold. You want your husband to worship the ground you walk on and think that you alone bring the sun to rise each day, yes?"

The young girl thought for a moment. "Why, yes. I suppose that I do."

Penelope blossomed with her rapt audience. She rather felt like some manner of professor, or maybe an actress on the stage. "Well, sometimes, men need a bit of help to realize what they have. This is why we are to be delicate roses, so beautiful to look on, they fear that their merest breath would cause the flower to wilt and that any touch besides the most gentle might cause them to be pricked by thorns. That is how we, not men, actually make a marriage."

Flora nodded, seeming captivated by all Penelope had told her. Penelope made a mental note to write those last words down. She always jotted down her daily happenings in her diary, and she felt that her little tale about the rose was rather good.

As the carriage stopped, the girls hopped out, entering the hotel to a flurry of introductions and greetings. Everyone who was anyone took their tea at the Stoneward at least once a week. Penelope, seeing herself as a bit of a trendsetter, strived to go twice.

"Penelope, dear, do introduce us to your friends!" Greta Hallstone, followed by two of her closest minions, practically ran up to Penelope as they made their way to their table.

"Greta, this is Lady Flora MacLeod and her cousin Mister Drummond MacGregor," Penelope said in her more careful hostess voice. "Flora, Mister MacGregor, this is Greta Hallstone of the East End Hallstones."

"Charmed." Greta held out a gloved hand to Drummond MacGregor who took it gently and dipped a small bow. Greta looked back at her underlings and raised her brows. "Oh, my, a bow and everything! I suppose they *do* teach manners in Scotland, after all."

Greta's followers giggled behind their fans, Flora blushed, and MacGregor stayed completely still. Penelope, however, could not stay silent.

"Oh, Greta," she crooned, a sugary-sweet smile on her lips. "They *do* teach manners in Scotland. But it's a shame they do not in the East End."

Greta froze, mouth hanging open in shock. "Why, I…I…"

"Do take care now, darling." She patted Greta on the arm, then motioned for Flora and MacGregor to follow her. "Come, now, we don't want to be late for tea."

"Oh, my goodness," Flora hissed excitedly. "Did you see the look on her face when you said that?"

"Don't turn around and look at her again. We want her to think that *we* don't give her a second thought." Penelope took her seat at a round table by the window, Flora on her left and MacGregor on her right. "Greta's always been a hag."

"Does she dislike Scottish people?" MacGregor asked, breaking his usual silence.

"She dislikes everyone," Penelope said simply as a waiter approached. "We're not special."

Chapter Four

Penelope powdered her nose a final time, then rose from her dressing table. It was almost time for her birthday ball and she could barely contain her frayed nerves. Not even the warm cup of invigorating tea a maid had brought her earlier did much to quell her irrational fears. She tried to focus on the familiar, instead of the unknown.

She recalled all the other parties and dances she and Charlotte had prepared for together over the years in her relatively unchanged bedroom. Almost every week, Charlotte would come to Penelope's house to have her hair dressed, face powdered, and gown buttoned up before the pair would set off to the latest society event.

But no matter how comforting her chambers were, she couldn't stop the pattering of her heart. "What if everything goes wrong?" She sighed.

"Nothing will go wrong," Charlotte promised. "You look divine, the guests have all arrived, and I do believe I saw some rather lovely gifts piling up for you in the entryway."

She inspected herself in her full-length mirror. She wore a gown of the palest blue, a shade that flattered her creamy skin and pale, blonde hair, set in a series of rolled curls piled upon her head, with loose coils falling down her back. The dress had been carefully made in Paris. From under the wide pickups peeked white lace, hung in place by light pink silk roses.

"I do suppose I look like quite the lady tonight, do I not?"

Charlotte nodded. "A most fine example of an English Rose."

"Father always did say I rather resembled a young Elizabeth Woodville."

"Who?"

"Elizabeth Woodville, the wife of King Edward IV. You read more than a professor does. Surely, you know who I'm speaking of?"

"I haven't done much reading, of late."

"Well, she was a widowed mother of two sons when she made Edward IV fall madly in love with her. She was a common woman who was so beautiful that she turned the head of a king."

"Penelope," Charlotte began, placing a hand on her friend's shoulder, "you are anything but common. Now, enough with the history lesson. Let's go find you a husband."

***

As the two ladies glided down the grand staircase into the Elmsly ballroom, their names were announced by a footman in livery to the gathered guests.

"Miss Penelope Elmsly, daughter of the Baron Elmsly, and Lady Charlotte MacLeod."

The Elmsly ballroom was not the largest in London, and it had once been described as rather cozy, but it was now decorated immaculately in a glaze of blushing roses and white linen. Edmund and Cecily had not spared any expense when planning the event. Waiters in livery shuttled sweets and wine about the room, which was lit with hundreds of candles in golden candelabras.

"It is a nice turn out, don't you think, darling?" Cecily asked, appearing suddenly at her daughter's elbow, her eyes sharp.

"Lovely," Penelope answered, already counting the number of men swarming around her, sharks in the presence of a marriageable heiress.

"Miss Elmsly, may I introduce myself? I am Franklin Harrison," the first interjected over the din. He was a rail thin man with more teeth than face.

Ever the hostess, Penelope set out her hand to be kissed. "Thank you so much for attending my birthday ball."

"I could never refuse an invitation from your ravishing mother." Franklin grinned, making him appear quite horse-like.

Penelope shifted her eyes toward Charlotte, who hid a bout of laughter with a delicate cough behind her fan.

"Oh, you're too much, Mister Harrison." Cecily's round cheeks reddened.

"Allow me to introduce my brother." Franklin motioned to the man at his side. "Theodore

Harrison, the proprietor of the Atlantic Star Shipping Company," he added with a look of exaggerated modesty.

Theodore grazed Penelope's fingers. "How do you do?"

"Quite well, and yourself?" Her voice was soft with surprise. Theodore and Franklin hardly looked like brothers. Where Franklin was all gums, fangs, and flourish, Theodore was classically handsome. He possessed a straight nose, carefully parted light brown hair, a dashingly dimpled chin, and a pair of warm brown eyes that did not stray from her face as they met.

"Much better now that I am home in England," he replied smoothly.

"My brother has just returned from the East indies," Franklin said proudly. "He saw all sorts of savages and wild things, but has brought back quite the variety of exotic goods."

Cecily raised a brow, a habit given to her only daughter. "How interesting. You know, my husband owns The Piccadilly Emporium."

Franklin pressed a hand to his chest, feigning shock. "What a coincidence. Did you hear that, Theodore?"

"Yes. I actually have a meeting with Baron Elmsly next week," Theodore explained, finally looking away from Penelope. "I was hoping to make a trade agreement, if he finds my wares up to snuff."

"I have no doubt my husband will be enamored with all of your wondrous commodities." Cecily nodded her head. "Yes, yes. Edmund, my husband, has always been captivated by the Indies. He would have served Her Majesty's army in the colonies, had he the chance. But he got his mother's knobby knees!"

"Then I'm sure we will have much to discuss at our meeting," Theodore said with a small smile. "If you ladies will excuse me, I see a business associate I must speak with. Might the lady of the hour spare me a dance this evening?"

"Of course. I'll place you on my dance card presently," Penelope promised, watching as Theodore and Franklin disappeared into the crowd.

"The proprietor of the Atlantic Star Shipping Company," Cecily whispered as she dug her nails into Penelope's arm. "You could do worse."

"He did seem rather nice," Charlotte said. "And he was very handsome."

"He was, wasn't he?" Penelope penned his name on her card for one of the longer waltzes.

"Penelope! Charlotte!" Flora pushed through the ton, positively glowing in a dark purple gown.

"We were wondering where you were." Charlotte smiled. "I thought you were coming early to dress with us?"

"I was, but I dropped a hot roller onto my first gown last night while selecting which jewels to wear, so I had to run out today and find a replacement." Flora looked toward Penelope. "Who was that man I saw you speaking with?"

"The proprietor of the Atlantic Star Shipping Line," Cecily said with a raised voice.

"Mother, how many times will you say 'the proprietor of the Atlantic Star Shipping Line'?"

Penelope giggled. "You're very much like an advert in the back of a novel."

Cecily huffed. "Don't poke fun, I think it's a fine profession. Now, I'm going to go find your father and speak with him about this meeting with Theodore Harrison." She waved a small goodbye and hurried off to plot and plan with her husband."

"Theodore Harrison? Is that the man?" Flora questioned.

"The very same," Charlotte said, pulling out her elaborate fan and fluttering it gently, making her hair move. "Penelope's mother seemed quite fond of him."

"Don't fret, my mother will find fault with him soon enough." She straightened up into an overdramatically proper stance, taking on a higher-pitched tone. "Theodore Harrison? Oh, goodness, no! His eyes are too close together and I noticed three freckles on his cheek! He's obviously a murderer and a thief."

Charlotte let out a snort. "That sounds *so* much like your mother."

"What do you think of him?" Flora was craning her neck to peer over the guests.

Penelope shrugged. "He's handsome and owns a rather prosperous business. I can't say for certain if he's my type, though."

"You could do worse," Charlotte mimicked Cecily.

"Do stop it," Penelope scolded with a smile. "He seems to be one of the better looking gentlemen in attendance, though."

"But would he make a fine husband? Do you

think he could fulfill all of your qualifications?"

"Honestly, how could I say? I've only just met the man!"

"Oh, here comes Drummond." Charlotte's hazel eyes widened. "He certainly looks rather striking this evening."

"Charlotte, do you *ever* stop teasing?" She glared at her, much to Flora's amusement.

"Lady Charlotte, Lady Flora, Miss Penelope." MacGregor nodded to each in turn before focusing on Penelope. "Happy birthday."

"Thank you, Mister MacGregor." She smiled. Although she wouldn't dare admit it, he *did* cut a fine figure in his kilt and jacket. His rugged good looks could charm a snake. If only his bland personality could measure up to his muscular form and graceful quietness.

"Lady Charlotte, Lord MacLeod sent me to find ye. He's only just arrived and is waitin' by the entrance for ye."

"Oh, thank you, Drummond. I'll go to him presently." Charlotte winked at Penelope and snapped her fan shut before leaving to see her husband. Flora slipped off silently at her heels, looking over her shoulder in that playful MacLeod way.

"How are you finding your time in London, Mister MacGregor?" Penelope asked.

"It's a fine place to visit, but I'd like to be in Scotland all the more."

"I've never been, but I've promised Charlotte I'd come and visit her often. At this point, I might as well move there with her." She laughed a bit, thinking inwardly of growing old into a spinster in Scotland, a gaggle of sheep to keep her company in lieu of the traditional cats. She could take up knitting and become an old crone in the castle, the witch of legends.

He studied her for a moment, bright green eyes taking in her amused expression. Penelope acquired that strange feeling, once again, that he could see into a secret part of her that even she did not know of. It sent a peculiar chill up her spine and when she saw a familiar face in the crowd, she took advantage.

"Do excuse me," Penelope began, "but I see an old friend of my brother's and I really must go say hello."

MacGregor bowed as she turned away and hurried over to where her brother's school friend, Charlie, stood grinning as she approached.

"The lady of the hour!" Jolly natured Charlie greeted her, sloshing drink from his cup in his hurry to press her hand.

"Charlie, it's so good to see you!" She meant it. He was almost like another brother to her, having spent many vacations at her country home with her brothers whenever school was out of session. Certainly, he had spent a lot of that time playing dolls with her, but it made her love the jovial man all the more to have seen his soft side.

"I could never miss a party in your honor."

"But to come all this way? I'm flattered."

His freckled face drew near, obviously ready for a tidbit of gossip. "But, I must ask, who is that large man you were speaking with? Rather a big fellow, but very handsome. Or, what is it the Scots say? *Bonny*?"

"Yes, that's right. And I suppose he's good enough to look at, if you're attracted to that type." Penelope tried to sound unaffected, but it only seemed to make Charlie all the more interested.

"You mean you're not attracted to a strapping lad in a savage kilt?" He looked around, then leaned toward her. "I say, do you know what Scots wear beneath their kilts?"

Penelope choked down a laugh and slapped him with her fan. "Do hush before you embarrass yourself. As I was about to ask, do you remember my friend Charlotte?"

"Of course! She ran off to Scotland with a lord. Rather explosive business," Charlie said, his cheeks pinking. "Rather *exciting* business, at that."

"Well, he's one of Conner MacLeod's cousins. He's staying in London as a male chaperone to Lady Flora MacLeod, Conner's sister."

"Is that the *only* reason he's staying in London?"

"Whatever do you mean?" Penelope asked.

Charlie's brows disappeared into his mop of red hair. "Surely you've noticed how he looks at you? One might assume you're *involved*."

Penelope shook a finger at Charlie. "I know you're fishing for a morsel of juicy chatter, but I'll tell you now there's none to be had."

"If you say so," he mumbled into his goblet of wine. "But, as an uninvolved third party, I must say that I wouldn't give it a second thought if you were to take him for *a turn about the room*."

She gasped, her cheeks burning. "Charlie, you're

shameful."

"Oh, you love it!" He took another gulp and perked up as his eye met something in the crowd. "I say, here comes Theodore!"

Theodore Harrison made his way toward them, nodding at Penelope as he entered their space. "Miss Penelope, I didn't know you knew Charles."

"Oh, yes," Charlie said eagerly, eyeing Theodore with appreciation. "I was at school with Penelope's bothers, Samuel and John. We've been as family for many years."

"Well, then, I hope you won't mind if I come to collect your foster sister for a dance?"

Charlie waved a hand dismissively. "Oh, no, please do!"

Theodore turned to Penelope and extended his hand. "Miss Penelope, may I?"

"Of course." She placed her hand in his, allowing him to lead her onto the dance floor.

Theodore proved to be a skilled dancer. His level of smooth movement was one born of careful education and constant use. Penelope appreciated that he took obvious care in his dancing, as well as his physical appearance.

Theodore wore a perfectly cut dark evening coat with tails and a deep green vest, topped off with a paisley ascot. This impeccable suit, paired with his handsome face and appropriate height, made him a fine match for Penelope's English Rose appearance.

"Are you enjoying your evening, Miss Elmsly?" Theodore questioned, his face placid and calm.

"Quite." She noticed how his voice sounded strong and firm. She appreciated his steady pitch.

"How did you find the Indies?"

He paused a moment in contemplation. "Extremely hot, but altogether it was a fine trip that I look forward to making again."

"It sounds ever so exotic. I do love hearing about faraway lands and the interesting cultures within them. Have you had the chance to visit anywhere else?"

"Not outside the usual France and Germany. I was hoping to see Spain later this year. I heard the coastline is most beautiful."

The song ended and the next began, but Penelope stayed in Theodore's arms. Out of the corner of her eye, she spied her mother, watching them closely with an odd look upon her face. Penelope recognized the expression. The gears within her mother's head were turning at a rapid pace, which wasn't always a good thing.

"Are you all right, Miss Elmsly?" His forehead creased in concern.

She pinked a bit, embarrassed to have let her mind wander. "Oh, quite all right, I merely saw my mother in the crowd."

"She is a lovely woman. By the time I had given my regards to your father, she had already sung my praises." He seemed rather pleased by this fact.

"Well, that doesn't sound quite like my mother," she mumbled to herself.

"Would you care to take a turn about the room?" he asked, offering an arm.

Penelope placed her hand upon it, smiling up at his eager face. "Do you plan on staying in London long?"

"Perhaps," he said as they passed a group of chaperones that nodded in mass approval upon seeing the pair. "I have a bit of business to take care of in the city, but I could stay longer, if I wished."

"Do you have a home in the city?"

"Two, actually." He cleared his throat. "One near the theater district and another closer to the finer residential area."

Penelope took a mental note. "And the country? Do you find yourself spending much time there?"

"Not as of late. I was hoping to purchase a small estate, once I'm settled down." His voice had an odd lift as he spoke. "Do you find the country agreeable?"

"Quite. My father has a country home that we often spend our summers at."

"I must speak with him, then. Perhaps he could help me find an agreeable piece of land to build upon."

"I'm sure he would be more than happy to help."

"Surely you have other callers to check off your dance card," he said as their circle of the room sent them back toward Cecily. "I can't monopolize the birthday girl's entire evening. Although, I would like to have another dance later, if I may?"

"That would be lovely, Mister Harrison. Thank you." Penelope smiled as he left her with her mother.

"So?" Cecily gripped her arm, bringing her face closer. "Tell me everything."

Her eyes widened. "Mother, really. We've barely spoken."

"You had a dance and a stroll. That's more than

enough time to decide if you like him. So, do you?"

"He's nice enough, handsome, owns two homes in the city, looking for land in the country, and owns a thriving business. He certainly checks off many of the requirements. I promised him another dance."

"Good, this is good." Cecily let go of her and tapped her chin with her fan. "Perhaps he'll call on you tomorrow? No, too soon."

Penelope scanned the room, catching sight of Charlotte speaking with one of the other women. "I'll speak with you later," she told her mother before scurrying around the dance floor toward her friend.

"Thank goodness I've found you. My mother is insane."

"You've just now noticed?" Charlotte giggled.

"I must get away from her. She's driving me wild."

"Come by for dinner tomorrow. I was thinking of having a bit of a supper. Nothing terribly fancy. I just hoped to spend some more time with everyone before we return to Scotland."

"You're not leaving soon, are you?"

"As soon as the children's home opens, we have to return. We'll have been gone almost three months by then and Conner really needs to get back."

Penelope pouted dramatically. "However shall I survive without you here?"

"I have faith in you. Will you come for dinner?"

"Of course. Who else will be there?

Charlotte waved a hand. "It's only us."

"Who is us?"

"Conner, Flora, Drum, you, and me. Merely a small party with the nearest and dearest. But tell me about Theodore Harrison. You looked as if he was amusing enough."

"He might have checked all the boxes," Penelope said behind her fan. "Handsome, moneyed, two town homes and plans to buy in the country. He's also quite an easy conversationalist."

"So, he is a prospect?"

Penelope spied her mother stalking toward Theodore with Edmund in tow. "More like prey."

Chapter Five

Penelope came to the MacLeod home promptly at eight the next evening dressed in a new peach gown. The butler led her to the drawing room where the rest of the party was waiting, drinks in their hands.

"Penelope, you look lovely in that color." Flora smiled as she entered.

"Thank you," Penelope pressed Flora's hand and took an offered wine glass from a footman. "I'm so pleased to be able to dine with all of you."

"It certainly would no' be a dinner party without ye." Conner tipped his cup toward her, one arm around Charlotte's waist.

"Mister MacGregor, I hope the evening finds you well?" Penelope asked cordially. The silent Scot had been watching her from his spot near the fireplace.

"Verra well, Miss Elmsly." He tipped a small bow. "And yourself?"

She smiled. "I find myself exceptionally well, if not more than famished."

"Do no' fash." Conner glanced at a footman, who nodded at his lord. "Supper is ready now." He held out his arm for his wife, escorting her to the dining room, stopping only to offer his sister the other.

MacGregor held out an arm to Penelope, his green eyes taking her in. "Miss Elmsly?"

Penelope pinked under his gaze, but still placed a small hand on his elbow. She could feel each muscle under the thin fabric of his white shirt. Usually, men wore jackets at all times, not giving her the chance to feel much more than cloth. But MacGregor's skin was warm beneath her fingers and the steady heat almost seemed obscene in the oddest way. A fully clothed man shouldn't have that profound an affect upon her.

"Penelope," Charlotte called from one end of the long dinner table, "you're on my right, next to Drum."

MacGregor deposited her in her seat, carefully pulling out her chair. He then sat beside her. Flora took the seat opposite them while Conner was at the table's head. Flora shot Penelope the familiar mysterious MacLeod grin, her dark blue eyes then focusing on Charlotte, who returned the look with an equally cryptic smile.

"You set a beautiful table, Charlotte," Penelope said, trying to start an acceptable conversation.

"Thank you, but that wasn't my doing. It was all the work of our butler, John." She waved a hand at the man in livery who bowed his head.

"First course is turtle soup," Charlotte announced as footmen entered with bowls of steaming broth.

"How exotic!" Penelope exclaimed, picking up her spoon. She had sampled turtle soup only once before and found it delicious.

MacGregor peered down at the china bowl suspiciously.

"What's the matter, Drum?" Conner asked.

"Why would anyone care to eat a wee mud creature like the turtle?" MacGregor questioned, dipping his spoon into the soup.

"Just give it a try," Conner prodded.

MacGregor hesitantly sipped the soup. "Interestin'."

Charlotte giggled. "Merely interestin'?"

"I'll take a fine cut o' meat above a wee soup any day," Drum stated. "No' bad, though."

"Then you'll be pleased to hear that the cook has done up a fine lamb for the next course," Conner told him.

MacGregor smiled widely, showing off rows of perfectly white teeth. Penelope looked at him from the corner of her eye, noticing how different the Scotsman appeared when not on bodyguard duty. While he had always been handsome, the added mirth in his eyes made him seem softer, more approachable. It suited him well.

"Ach, here's the real food," MacGregor said as meat-laden dishes were laid upon the table. He stabbed a large piece, placing it on Penelope's plate before serving himself.

"Oh, thank you." Penelope glanced over at Charlotte, who suddenly seemed quite concerned with her wine. Thinking it a Scottish custom,

Penelope scooped up a pile of roasted potatoes, plopping them on MacGregor's dish. "There, now we're quite even."

He looked at her in amusement. "Even?"

"Yes," she said, cutting up her lamb. "You served me meat, so I served you something as well."

MacGregor let out a short laugh. "Ach, I merely thought ye needed the largest bit because it looks as if ye'd blow away."

Penelope bristled, covering it up with a smooth raise of an eyebrow. "Well, someone has come out of his shell since we last spoke."

"Ach, Drum means nothin' by it," Conner said, holding out his cup to be filled by a footman. "He's only bein' polite. Also, he's much more himself without the pryin' eyes o' the British ton. We all share food in Scotland."

"Understandable," she said, biting into the tender meat. "I can barely stand the scrutiny at times, but it is just the cost of being in society."

"I rather like society in England," Flora piped in. She'd become somewhat of a local darling, being invited to tea with some of the high-standing ladies and flipping through daily invitations to dinner parties and balls.

"It's easier for a woman to fit in than it is for a man," Charlotte pointed out.

"Aye. Sometimes people look at me like I'd devour their first-born. But I always say that English babes are too tough for my likin'," MacGregor added with a booming laugh.

"I think that's deplorable," Penelope stated.

"You're a perfect gentleman and they have no right to look down on you merely because you're quite…" She narrowed her eyes, trying to think of a word to describe his massive size. "Big."

"Big?" MacGregor echoed, his lips quivering with amusement.

"Well, Drum's no' just a large lad," Conner said with a lopsided grin. "He has a right fine voice, as well."

"Ach, do no' do it," MacGregor moaned, putting down his fork.

"But ye must," Conner replied in all seriousness.

Penelope turned to Charlotte. "What is Conner making Mister MacGregor do?"

"Oh, do stop calling him Mister MacGregor," Charlotte said. "It's very strange to hear."

Penelope rolled her eyes. "And calling someone I hardly know by their first name would be exceptionally rude."

"You're going to see a lot of him, going forward, as he's Flora's chaperone. Might as well get better acquainted." Charlotte sipped her wine. "Scottish home, Scottish customs, in any case."

"Aye." MacGregor agreed. "I do no' think o' myself as Mister MacGregor."

Penelope paused. "Well, I suppose it would save time to cut right to a first name basis, as long as we don't make a habit of such impropriety while in public. After all, I did implore you to call me Penelope."

"Come now, Drum. We can no' have a true dinner party among friends without ye spinnin' a song." Conner slapped his hand upon the table. "A song!"

MacGregor shrugged his broad shoulder. "Aye, I suppose I must."

"Is there a lot of singing at Scottish dinners?" Penelope asked Charlotte.

Charlotte nodded. "Yes, there's usually some form of entertainment—musicians, pipers, singers."

"How novel."

MacGregor didn't seem to have any sort of stage fright as he rose to stand behind his chair. "Any requests?"

"*Ba Mo Leanabh*!" Flora exclaimed, shifting in her seat with excitement. "It's been weeks since I've heard a proper Scottish tune."

"All right." MacGregor cleared his throat, taping out a few beats before he began to sing.

Penelope listened, enraptured. The words were unlike any she was familiar with but the mournful melody of his steady voice sent a chill up her spine. MacGregor crooned softly, picking up the tempo at times, perfectly conveying emotion with the tone of his words. The song was hauntingly beautiful. It was almost unbelievable that the enchanting sound was coming from such a giant's lips.

When he finished, she let out a deep breath she hadn't been aware she was holding. "That was.... Amazing." She sighed.

Flora and Charlotte clapped in unison, stealing conspiratorial looks from behind their hands.

"Thank ye," MacGregor said, beginning to sit back down.

"What was it?" Penelope asked, still feeling the effects of the music.

"It's an old song from my family. There was a man who wanted to claim the throne, Gregor MacGregor. He fought against the Campbells and was killed for it. His widow was said to be so distraught by his untimely demise, she wrote *Ba Mo Leanabh* for her children. It's mainly a lullaby now, but it used to be almost a call to arms for my clan, while there was one."

Penelope leaned forward. "What happened?"

"By the 1600s, bein' a MacGregor was punishable by death." He turned in his seat to face her. "Most renounced their clan, others were hanged, some laid in wait for two hundred years."

"Aye," Conner interjected. "Drum's one o' the last. Now the MacGregors are workin' on havin' their clan recognized again."

"How can they outlaw a name?" Charlotte asked.

"The same way the English outlaw the kilts and the bagpipes and anythin' else Scottish they do no' like." Conner patted Drum's arm. "Aye, Drum's family are a bunch o' holdouts."

"Will you sing another, Drum?" Flora pleaded. "That song made me ever so homesick."

He pursed his lips. "Aye, somethin' a bit for fun, then?"

They sat together for hours around the table, sharing bits of food as MacGregor took requests, most of which were in Scottish Gaelic. Nonetheless, Penelope found herself entranced when he sang, hanging on each word and always hoping for more.

"Shall we move to the drawin' room?" Conner stretched. "I fancy a nip o' whiskey to end out my evenin'."

They retired to the drawing room where their night had begun and Penelope found herself standing by the fireplace, MacGregor seated to her right. With him sitting down, they were nearly the same height.

"I must say, Mister MacGregor, you have a wonderful voice."

"None o' that, now." He took a drink from the crystal decanter in his hand. "We've shared food and song. Call me Drummond."

"Very well, Drummond, where did you learn to sing like that?"

"No' sure, to be true. Many o' the clan's legends and songs were passed down generations and landed with me." He laughed. "Tis a shame there are no' more o' us to share the stories with."

"What about writing them down? Books of family history and song are all the rage, currently. My father's store has dozens."

He scratched his chin thoughtfully, bringing his scarred knuckles into view. "No' a bad idea to write down what I know. But I doubt somethin' like that would find itself in a London shop."

"I'm not saying you need to be a famous author, but wouldn't it be something to share those songs with others?"

"Aye, that it would be."

"Shall I fetch some papers and a pen? You should start now and get it all written down as it's fresh," she suggested eagerly. "I'm sure my father knows dozens of publishers. Maybe just get a few printed and bound. I know I've even seen a few Scottish-looking names in the shops."

He shifted from one foot to the other. "That's a lot to think about."

"Please take what I've said into consideration. I know I would love to read a book of songs so beautiful with instrumental accompaniment. You could add in sheet music, as well. But perhaps consider an English translation for each Scottish song."

Drummond smiled, but leaned in closer, lowering his head slightly. "To be true, the Gaelic would no' be the problem."

Penelope knitted her brow. "Then what is?"

He grimaced. "I do no' know how to write music and I do no' think I could write it well in English. Gaelic and Latin were all we were taught in the church schools."

"Oh, posh." Penelope waved a hand. "You can't let something so ridiculous stop you. I'll help you write it. Once Charlotte and Conner leave to go back to Scotland, I'll be spending a lot of time with Flora. We can work on it a bit then."

"Aye, that could work well, but I'd hate to put ye out so."

"What are you two whispering about, over there?" Charlotte called from the far end of the room where she sat with Conner and Flora.

"Drummond and I are writing a book," Penelope said primly, fluffing out her skirts.

"A book?" Conner looked incredulous. "Ach, Drum, I did no' know ye could read!"

"Aye, I'm no' just a pretty face," Drummond retorted, causing them all to laugh.

Penelope glanced at the gifted clock on the

mantelpiece. "Oh, dear, it's nearly midnight!"

"That late already?" Charlotte yawned and glanced up at Conner slyly. "Well, I do think we should go up soon."

"Aye, I'm suddenly verra tired." Conner stretched dramatically, ever one for the theatrics.

Flora handed her cup to a footman. "Won't you stay, Penelope?"

"I would if I could. But my parents will worry if I'm not home and I don't wish for a maid to wake them with a message."

"Then you must come to stay when Charlotte and Conner leave. I'll be so lonely all by myself." Flora pouted.

"Aye, I suppose I'm just a chair then?" Drummond asked. "Or a wee footstool?"

Flora scoffed. "Don't be so dramatic. You know what I mean. You're not exactly a prime conversationalist."

"I'll call for a carriage, Miss Elmsly," a footman muttered before scuttling off toward the great hall.

As Penelope said her goodbyes, she found she was rather sad to leave the jolly family full of song and laughter. As the last child, and a surprise one at that, she had never known a home full of boisterous meals and close siblings. She supposed that's why she had bonded so well with Charlotte, an only child herself. The idea of going back to the quiet Elmsly townhouse didn't seem very appealing.

"I will hold you to the promise of some sleepovers," Penelope told Flora as she readied herself to leave. Charlotte and Conner had already excused themselves, rushing up the stairs in a cloud of muffled laughter and silks.

"Please do!" Flora grinned.

"It will give us time to work on your book of music and history," Penelope said pointedly to Drummond. "So, begin to think about what you would like to include."

"Aye, mistress."

Penelope rolled her eyes. "No need for your cheek. I'll see you both soon."

She entered the carriage and sat back in the seats, thinking about her evening. She had felt very welcome with the Scottish family, more so than at most English dinner parties. Flora was adorable as always, Charlotte and Conner were a nauseating mess of hormones, but she saw a new side to the gentle giant Drummond.

While she once thought him a mindless soldier incapable of deeper thought, she had been remarkably surprised by the depth of his musical talents and how amusing he could be. Behind closed doors he was positively charming as well as handsome. It was a pity he was nothing more than a Scottish fighter and not a titled man with money, like Conner.

"Yes," Penelope whispered to herself as the horses drew the carriage down the narrow London roads. "What a pity."

Chapter Six

The day was dreary when Penelope awoke. Not bothering to dress, she donned a pale green wrapper and descended to breakfast, her hair still braided from sleep.

"Good morning, darling," Edmund said as he flipped through a newspaper.

"Good morning mother, Father." Penelope slid into her seat, stifling a yawn as a footman placed a cup of tea and a plate before her. She immediately took a bite of sausage. "Any post for me?"

"I thought you'd never ask!" Cecily handed her an envelope, eagerly watching as Penelope slid it open with a butter knife.

"Oh, it's from Theodore Harrison," Penelope said.

Miss Penelope Elmsly,

If you would be so inclined, I would wish to make a formal call upon your home this afternoon.

Your dutiful servant,
Theodore Harrison

Penelope turned it over. "Rather a short letter."

"Theodore Harrison is coming *here*?" Cecily tapped her fingers on the table. "There's so much to do."

Penelope poured milk into her tea, watching her mother fret with interest. "Pass the sugar, please?"

"Sugar? How can you think about sugar when Theodore Harrison is coming to call?"

Edmund looked up at them over the edge of his paper. "He's the young chap with the India contracts, yes?"

"Yes!" Cecily pushed the sugar toward Penelope.

"Nice lad," Edmund murmured, flipping the page. "I say, it says here there's a new railway heading back toward our country estate. That will make our travels much easier."

Cecily heaved a loud sigh. "Edmund, this is important. We must be prepared."

"What's there to be prepared for? He's a social caller, just as the rest of them," he said.

"Edmund, dear," Cecily's practiced voice was clear and steady, "this isn't just some regular gentleman caller, it is *the* gentleman caller. So, in order to receive him, we must all be ready. See if you can end your business early so that you might be home when he comes." She turned to her daughter. "And, Penelope, wear your pink silks, the one with the black trimming."

"You'd think we were having tea with a king," Edmund grumbled, folding up his paper and placing it on the table. "I'm off to work."

Penelope watched the proceedings, nibbling her toast. As soon as he father left, her mother began fretting over tea arrangements.

"What to do, what to do?" Cecily wailed, shaking the bell at her side.

The butler came from a side door. "Yes, Madam?"

"We are having Theodore Harrison for tea this afternoon."

"Mother, he only said he was going to call, not that he was coming to tea," Penelope pointed out.

Cecily ignored her. "I need the cook to prepare something exquisite for this afternoon. Cakes, sandwiches, the finest Arabian teas…or perhaps the Chinese. Use your best judgment."

"Yes, Madam." The butler left to carry out his orders, leaving the two Elmsly women together.

Penelope pushed her plate away. "I suppose I should go primp and prepare?"

"Please do." Cecily sighed. "Theodore is the most eligible bachelor in London. Everyone has been pushing their daughters onto him. It's positively shameful."

Penelope chose to ignore her mother's hypocrisy and left the breakfast room to return to her quarters for a long bath. Once in her rooms, she saw that a maid had already filled the tub, adding lavender oils to the fragrant water.

She dropped her dressing robe and pulled off her nightgown, pausing only to pin up her hair. The water was still hot as she submerged her body, allowing the lavender to relax her. She briefly wondered if she should feel as anxious for Theodore Harrison's visit as her mother was. After all, the man would be calling for Penelope, and not her parents.

However, he wasn't the first man to call upon her. The past two years had been filled with a bevy of gentlemen coming to court and being promptly turned away for some insignificant reason by her mother. Penelope wasn't overly fond of any of the men, but wondered if Theodore Harrison would be the one to change her feelings. She longed for a beautiful wedding to a darling man and a gaggle of adorable children and he seemed just the one to fit her ideal mate.

Penelope's mind wandered from daydreams of a fine country home with a noble husband to a fine country home with Drummond MacGregor as her husband. She felt her face grow hot at the thought of him seated before an estate fireplace, a series of blond, green-eyed children at his feet. She nearly laughed out loud in embarrassment at the mere idea, more to cover the faint sense of contentment it gave her than actual mortification.

After her bath, she called in a maid to dress her and tend to her hair. Once she was deemed suitable for callers, she returned downstairs to the drawing room where her piano was kept. From a young age, Penelope was a proficient musician and relished an opportunity to play new music. For that reason, she was itching to get her hands on those Scottish tunes she was promised.

She passed several hours at her cabinet pianoforte, going over the most recent sheet music

The Piccadilly Emporium had to offer. Penelope hardly noticed when the afternoon was upon her and was quite surprised when her mother rushed in, patting her graying curls into place.

"Hurry!" Cecily hissed, draping herself into am armchair and pulling an abandoned embroidery project into her lap. "Look productive!"

"I was being productive." She closed up her piano.

Cecily waved her over. "Sit there and pick up that book."

Penelope grabbed the novel in a pile on the side table. "This is a history of early whaling ships."

"Goodness, me, we're doomed."

"Do calm down, you're getting terribly flushed."

Cecily held a hand to her cheek. "Never you mind. Just sit down. I've had a maid on the lookout and he's coming down the walk right this moment and your father isn't even here!"

Penelope settled herself in her mother's matching armchair, adjusting her skirts with a practiced hand. She had just opened her whaling book to a thrilling chapter on harpoons when the butler entered after a short knock.

"A Mister Theodore Harrison to see Miss Elmsly. Shall I let him in?"

"Please do," Cecily answered, her voice once again calm and collected.

Several moments later, the butler reentered with Theodore Harrison at his heels. Cecily perked up immensely upon seeing him. Penelope thought she would jump out of her skin and marry him herself, given the chance.

"Mrs. Elmsly, Miss Elmsly." Theodore bowed as the women stood. "I am so honored to have been given the opportunity to call upon you this afternoon."

"The pleasure is ours," Penelope replied, holding out a hand.

He took it gently, bowing over it. "Miss Elmsly, you look a perfect flower on this cheerless day."

Penelope heard Cecily snap open a fan behind her and begin to flutter it frantically. She ignored her and turned to Theodore. "Thank you, Mister Harrison, you are too kind."

"And Mrs. Elmsly." Theodore crossed over to Penelope's mother and took her hand. "Lovely as always."

"Oh, Mister Harrison!" Cecily's cheeks were red and she shielded her face with her fan.

"Please, have a seat." Penelope motioned toward the couch before taking a seat upon her chair. She rang the bell, summoning tea. "Would you take refreshments?"

"Yes, thank you." Theodore sat on the couch, turned toward Penelope.

Two footmen entered, one carrying a tea tray, the other all manners of cakes and treats. Once they were all served, Cecily began the arduous task of general society niceties while Penelope silently sipped her tea.

"How have you been? How is your brother? The arcade is lovely. You must come visit. How is your tea?"

Only then could they get to the real reason why Theodore came to call.

"Miss Elmsly," Theodore finally addressed her, "would you accompany me to Hyde Park Thursday morning? The flowers in Kensington Gardens have been said to be at the peak of their bloom."

Cecily let a small squeal escape her pursed lips and attempted to cover it up with a small cough.

"That would be lovely, Mister Harrison," Penelope said with a gracious smile. "I've heard the gardens are quite lovely this time of year and have not had the pleasure of seeing them yet."

"Then I shall come at ten o'clock in the morning, if that would be agreeable?" Theodore asked, rising from his seat.

"Greatly," Penelope said sweetly.

He replaced his hat, tipping it at the women before following the butler from the room. As soon as the drawing room doors were shut, Cecily groaned, slumping down in her chair.

Penelope raised a brow. "Everything all right?"

"My dear, it is more than all right." Her eyes glistened.

"So, you actually approve of him?" She was surprised. Her mother found fault in every man who had ever sat upon that couch. "You don't think his head is an odd shape or that he's secretly a bank robber? You actually favor him?"

Cecily knitted her brow in confusion. "Of course, why wouldn't I? He's handsome, moneyed, charming. A mother's dream."

She stifled a laugh at her mother's eccentricities and slipped from the room to spare herself more dramatics and badgering. Once safely behind her closed bedroom doors, she allowed herself ponder how strange it was that Theodore was her mother's dream for her. She had to wonder if he was *her* dream, as well.

Chapter Seven

Penelope marched up the steps of the MacLeod townhome, blank music sheets and a new bottle of ink following her by way of a footman. She was led into the library where Flora sat before the fireplace, a small book in her hand.

"Good morning, Penelope." She grinned, marking her place in the novel and shutting it.

"Good morning. Where is everyone?"

"Charlotte and Conner have gone to the children's home to prepare for the opening on Saturday. You'll be there, yes?"

"Of course, although I'll be quite sad, as it marks the end of their stay here." She took her supplies from the footman and placed them upon the desk. "And Drummond?"

"He's around here, somewhere." Flora beckoned the footman. "Summon Drummond, if you will?"

"I don't want to bother him."

Flora's blue eyes flashed. "Oh, trust me, it won't bother him in the slightest."

Penelope ignored her and busied herself with

unpinning her fashionably feathered hat. She had just placed it next to her sheet music when Drummond entered, rolling his sleeves up to his elbows.

"Penelope, I hope the day finds ye well?"

"Substantially better now that I've found something to do. I was hoping you would have time to work on your manuscript today?"

He paused for a moment before answering, with a small glance toward Flora. "Aye, I do."

"Fantastic." Penelope gathered up the paper and ink. "I assumed there's some manner of piano somewhere?"

"Oh, yes, in the ladies' drawing room. Drummond knows where it is," Flora said, picking up her book again.

"Will you not come with us?" Penelope asked.

She didn't bother looking up from her pages. "Oh, no, I'm going to stay here and finish this novel. It's quite interesting."

Penelope rolled her eyes and looked at the large Scotsman. Propriety would demand she call for a maid to play chaperone, but as Drummond was basically an employee of the MacLeods, she didn't see the harm in being alone with him. There were many times when she'd been with a footman or butler without someone to oversee them. "Lead the way."

Drummond walked down the long hall, Penelope double stepping to keep up with his long strides. He opened a door near the end, motioning for her to enter first. This room was smaller than the regular drawing room with only one small fireplace, a piano, a settee, and a small writing desk. Drummond left the door open, something that didn't escape her attention.

She slid onto the piano stool and flipped up the mahogany top to reveal the keys. With no hesitation, she tested the keys with one of her favorite songs that she long ago had memorized. She was pleased to hear that the instrument was finely tuned. "Perfect. This shall do quite nicely."

"So, what are we to do now?" he asked, leaning back against the wall beside the piano. "I do no' know where to start."

"Well, I was thinking that we should go through some of the better known tunes you are familiar with, and go from there. I also thought that it might be smart to pick songs that have a backstory, as did the first one you sung at the dinner party."

"And ye can write the music?"

"Of course. All I need you to do is sing and talk. Let me take care of the rest." She smiled reassuringly and placed a blank sheet atop the piano and the tumbler of ink. "Oh, dash it all," she muttered as she realized she had forgotten a pen.

"Lookin' for one o' these?" Drummond had pulled one from his sporran and held it out to her, lips curled in amusement.

"You've read my mind," she said, taking the pen. "Now, let's begin. Sing it once and then I'll try to follow along with the piano."

He cleared his throat before beginning the haunting tune. Penelope listened hard, her fingers itching to touch the ivories. Once he had gotten through the first round, she motioned for him to begin again. This time, she attempted to mimic the flow of his voice with the sound of the keys.

"No' bad." Drummond nodded his head as she repeated her playing again for him to review. "Ye are rather good at this."

"I have an ear for music," she said plainly, dipping the pen in the ink. She made several marks upon the paper with one hand, the other slowly playing. "You will need to write down the words, though. I don't know what you're saying, nor do I know how to spell it."

"Do ye really think people would wish to read somethin' like this?" he asked, pulling out the desk's seat and placing it beside the piano.

"I do believe so," Penelope replied, looking up from her work. "If not, it's still nice for you to have for your people. History is often spun, when not properly recorded. We're basically historians."

Drummond sat down, his elbows upon his knees and his hands dangling. He watched as she wrote and Penelope could feel his eyes upon her. It almost felt unsettling, but at the same time, it was rather comforting to have such a gentle giant close at hand. While the dangers were limited in a drawing room in the fashionable side of London, aside from the terror of being served cold tea, Penelope still valued his competent company.

They worked with companionable ease that truly surprised her. She had never been so close to a man she was not related to—well, certainly not for so long and with such casual manners. If she was perfectly honest with herself, she would admit that those facts made her more nervous than she would like. Of course, nothing would occur between them, as Penelope had more sense than to be *too* familiar.

Drummond explaining the spellings and meanings of the Gaelic lyrics, while Penelope jotted down the notes and translations. After about an hour, she was pleased enough with their progress to move on to the next song in the book.

They were about to begin when Flora entered carrying a tea tray. "I thought you could use a break."

"Thank you." Penelope took a cup and held it out, allowing Flora to pour her some tea.

"Getting a lot done?" Flora asked, handing a piece of china to Drummond.

Penelope held in a laugh at the sight of the tiny teacup in his hand. She often forgot how large he was until moments such as that. "Yes, we've finished one already."

"Aye, Penelope has a way with the piano," Drummond told Flora.

Penelope pinked at his compliment and took a sip of tea, hoping the cup hid some of her face. "Well, Drummond has a way with song."

Flora made a small humming noise, her face unreadable. "I really must go upstairs. I have to go through my gowns and select something for Saturday."

"But you just got here," Penelope pointed out. She was becoming frustrated with Flora's constant need to cause mischief.

She placed her unfinished tea back on the tray. "Shall I send up something for you to nibble on?"

"Aye, this is hungry work." Drummond

stretched. "But somethin' a bit more substantial than wee cakes and sugared fruit."

"Of course." Flora glided form the room, leaving them alone again.

Penelope placed her cup back on its saucer and turned to Drummond. "So, what's next?"

He shrugged, leaning forward to look at her sheets of lyrics and notes. His face was close to hers then, and with his attention firmly on the papers, she could take a moment to see him, *really* see him.

Drummond had clear skin, tanned with hours of full sunlight. His lashes were dark, and his lips sat in a firm line as he read. Full, wavy hair brushed his shoulders, wonderfully tousled in a way that made him look both savage and carefree. The sleeves of his shirt were pushed up and she caught a glimpse of rough-looking skin. It was such a contrast to the rest of his flawless visible body that Penelope couldn't help but gawk.

"Frightenin', is it?" Drummond asked, looking at her intently under a heavy brow.

Penelope blushed and averted her eyes. "I'm sorry, that was exceptionally rude of me to stare so."

"Do no' fash." He pulled his sleeves down, covering the marred flesh. "Ye would no' be the first to stare."

"I really do apologize. It's not frightening. I'm just a discourteous fool."

"Perhaps that's enough for one day." He made a move to stand, but Penelope held out a hand, placing it upon his arm.

"Please, don't," she said, her cheeks still heated

with shame at humiliating him. "I feel terrible. Please forgive me."

He shifted in his seat, glancing down at her hand, so small compared to his. "Do no' think o' it. I'm sure the sight surprised ye."

"It did," she admitted. "But it isn't frightening. You must trust that I'm speaking true, as a genteel lady. As you know, a lady always faints upon seeing something *really* dreadful and I am the picture of health and stability at the present moment."

Drummond's serious façade cracked and his mouth turned into an amused grin. "Ye are a strange woman, Penelope."

"Well, that's not very polite, so I assume we're even," she said primly, taking her hand away from his arm and straightening her back.

"Should I show ye and get it over with?"

Penelope raised a brow. "What?"

"My scars. I can show ye so ye do no' have to wonder."

"I don't think that's truly necessary."

"But ye are curious?"

"A bit," she confessed quietly. "But I don't think that would be terribly proper."

"It's naught but a medical display," he said, rising form his seat. He unbuttoned several buttons at his throat before pulling the thin linin off.

Penelope immediately gasped and spun in her seat. Her body burned from her toes to her hair and her heart thumped wildly, knowing his naked torso was but a mere two feet away. Maybe even less. "Do get dressed before someone sees you!"

"Ye did no' even look."

"There's nothing to look at!"

"Well, that's rather rude," he mumbled with a laugh. "Just look and get it over with."

Penelope squared her shoulders and turned toward him. She saw immediately why he might feel insecure about his bare skin. His left arm, shoulder, and some of his chest were wrapped in the spidery scars, the kind left by burns. The skin was pink and puckered, obviously old, but not well-healed.

Drummond sat again and held out an arm for her closer inspection. "See? It frightens ye, I can tell by the way the blood left your face."

"But I haven't fainted," she said pointedly, trying to sound braver than she felt.

"That does no' mean ye would no', given the opportunity."

Tentatively, she reached out and brushed the marred skin with her fingers. It was warm beneath her palm and she squeezed lightly, trying to show that she wasn't afraid. "I'm *not* frightened," Penelope said softly but firmly, her eyes settling resolutely upon his. "It's just not every day someone strips before me."

He brushed his free hand through his hair, breaking their eye contact. "Ye'd be the first to no' be frightened."

"May I ask how this happened?"

"A few years ago we were raging against the MacKinney clan. They stole some horses, we stole them back along with some sheep. Normal disputes. But they took it too far and burned a small village, on the MacLeod lands, to the ground. I went to help put out the fires but got caught up in a barn while releasing the livestock. A beam had fallen on me and left me this way."

Penelope's brows knit with worry as her mind flashed to small baby cows and tiny sheep. "But what of the livestock?"

Drummond's brows shot up and he let out a booming laugh that made her jump. "*But what of the livestock…*" He doubled over in mirth, his hand on hers, anchoring her in place.

He seemed closer than before, as each of them teetered on the edges of their seats, their knees touching. Well, if Penelope was honest, they were more than just touching. Her legs were tucked between his and their faces were closer than was proper, as he was still bent low, trying to catch his breath. She smiled at the sight of him, so filled with humor. But she was still temped by the bare skin of his chest, almost made more ruggedly appealing by the scar. She could feel the twisted pattern of the burn beneath her fingers and almost wished she could feel the skin of his shoulder, his torso.

When Drummond saw her staring again, he paused, looking back at her between curtains of russet locks. His full lips parted and Penelope felt herself growing closer still, as if pulled by an invisible force. She waited for him to say something, a joke, or a smart remark. But she heard nothing more than her own heartbeat in her breast.

"Am I interrupting?" Flora asked from the doorway, her clever face impassable.

Penelope stood abruptly, nearly overturning the

piano stool with her bustled skirt. "Oh, no, we've just finished. I really must go home now."

"No need," Flora said. "I have much more to take care of. I was just seeing if you had been brought refreshments."

"Don't worry about it. I really must be going." She began gathering her things. "It must be getting terribly late."

"Please stay for supper," Flora implored, her face breaking into a ridiculous grin.

"I can't," she replied, attempting to take control of her flighty fingers that shook as she tried to carefully stack the sheets. "Drummond, top notch musical work, I'll be in touch about our scholarly pursuits."

"Should I see ye home, Penelope?" he asked, pulling his shirt back on.

"Oh, that won't be necessary." She avoided looking in his direction. "Goodbye! I'll see you both soon!"

She scurried from the house, leaving her hat behind.

Chapter Eight

Penelope was seated at her piano the next afternoon, perfecting the Scottish sheet music, when a footman entered.

"Miss Elmsly, there is a Mister MacGregor here to call upon you," the footman said. "He says he does not have a card to give you. Are you at home?"

"Oh, of course!" she blurted without thought. Penelope then cleared her throat, trying to look composed. Her mind raced as she wondered what the Scot had come for. Then she looked down at her piano, music and notes scattered upon the top. "Of course. He's here about the book."

Penelope dispelled the odd sting of regret as she closed up her instrument and gathered the papers. As she heard footsteps coming down the hall, she hurried over to a mirror, ensuring that her hair was still pinned neatly into its usual twisting bun.

"Mister MacGregor," the footman announced.

"Thank you." Penelope turned toward them. "Please bring us some refreshments."

The footman bowed and turned, exiting from the

room. Smiling, she motioned for Drummond to take a seat. He settled himself on the couch while she sat primly on her favorite armchair.

"I came to bring ye this. I hope it's no' a bad time." He held out a hatbox. "Flora told me ye had left it. She wanted to deliver it herself, but had another appointment."

"Oh, you didn't have to make a special trip just for this," Penelope said, taking the box and putting it by her feet for the footman to remove. "But, thank you all the same. I rather liked this particular hat."

"It's the least I could do, seein' as ye are helpin' me write the book and did no' run in horror upon seein' my scars."

Penelope averted her eyes from his emerald gaze, busying herself with straightening her skirts, a terrible nervous habit. "Please, don't mention it. I told you yesterday, and I'll tell you again, if I didn't faint at the sight of it, it wasn't all that horrifying. Really, Drummond, you think me so weak as to pass out at the sight of a little mark."

"No offence meant," he said with a smirk. "But I appreciate it, all the same."

"You know, you never did tell me what happened with the livestock," Penelope stated primly as a footman entered with tea and cakes.

Drummond covered up a laugh with a cough. "I'll know ye'll be pleased to hear that no pig was injured and all the wee piglets were safe from harm."

"I am glad to hear it," she said, passing him a teacup. "I would be rather vexed if you didn't have the fortitude to save all those innocent creatures."

The corners of his lips twitched and he waited until the footman had gone before speaking again. "Ye are a strange lass, Penelope Elmsly."

She raised a brow over the rim of her teacup. "No stranger than a giant Scotsman who runs about London delivering stray hats."

Penelope blushed at her own words. Usually she was so calm and collected, but the teasing words kept spilling from her mouth without abandon. Something about Drummond's presence opened her sharp mind and gave her outlet for the wit she usually only shared with Charlotte.

"I'll have ye know, your hats are the only ones in my charge."

While his words were innocent, as Penelope had only abandoned one of her dear accessories with him, his voice took on an odd lilt as he spoke. And, if she spoke true, she would say that it rather pleased her to know that Drummond wasn't traipsing about London. But that was none of her business. Not at all. Although she almost wished that it were.

She furrowed her brow as she held out a plate of treats to him, noting the peculiar look in his eyes as he gazed upon her. His green orbs always had a strange way of making her feel completely exposed, but she was slowly getting used to the new sensation.

Penelope cleared her throat, bringing the papers on the side table to his attention in an attempt to derail whatever was coming from their prolonged eye contact. "I've finished the final sheet music for some of your songs." She offered the pile to him, but he declined.

"Me lookin' at them makes no difference, seein' as I can no' read music. I trust ye."

"I suppose you can just go over them in the final works. All we need to do now, after compiling some more songs, is get the stories written down. I'm rather excited for that part."

"Well, I—"

"Penelope." Cecily was standing in the doorway, her face a mask of composure. "I was not aware you were currently entertaining."

"Mother, this is Drummond MacGregor, a cousin of Charlotte's husband," Penelope said as he shot up from his seat to greet Cecily. "Drummond, this is my mother, Cecily Elmsly."

"Pleasure to meet ye." Drummond made a slight bow.

Cecily returned the gesture with a tight-lipped smile. "And you. Penelope, could I steal you for just a moment?"

She nodded and followed her mother into the hallway, leaving Drummond standing by the fireplace. Cecily pulled her into the next room for privacy, closing the door behind her.

"Darling, why is there a large, kilted man sitting on my imported French settee?"

"I left my hat at the MacLeod home while visiting yesterday. He came to return it and we got caught up talking about the book we are compiling."

"Book? What book?"

"Drummond has a lovely voice and we're compiling the music and stories of his people into a book. It's really rather grand, the songs they have, and we don't have that much left to do before we'll be finished."

Cecily breathed hard through her nose. "And you're on a first name basis?"

"Apparently it's the way in Scotland when you share a meal. In public we always maintain propriety."

"Naturally," Cecily replied dryly. "You are aware, darling, how improper this looks? I wouldn't have any idea you were entertaining a man in a loincloth unless a maid had come for me."

Penelope silently cursed the unknown tattletale. "Mother, there's nothing improper about it," she said, ignoring the shirtless touching from the previous day. "What we're doing is a literary and historical feat. Besides, he's wearing a kilt, not a loincloth."

"You've entered the marriage market, Penelope, and while it was all well and good that Charlotte landed herself some kind of Scottish royalty, a romance in Scotland isn't in the cards for you."

She pinked, biting her lip in embarrassment. "Mother, this isn't a romance. We're just friends."

"Men and women can't be friends. Being friends with a man is how a lady gets with child and contracts disease."

She sighed. "Mother, you're being dramatic."

"I am not." Cecily held up a finger. "I won't have a daughter of mine being publicly courted by Theodore Harrison while privately entertaining a Scottish stranger."

"He's not a stranger."

"He will be." Her voice dropped low. "Make your excuses and send him away. You should know better than to entertain a man without a chaperone."

"But, Mother, we're—"

"No. He leaves at once. You're lucky your father is at the arcade. Otherwise the poor man would have a fit. No more visits, no more book, no more Scottish men!"

Penelope, shocked by her mother's harsh words and stern tone, left the room and came back to Drummond. Cecily stood in the doorway, once again the picture of calm sensibility.

"I'm sorry, there's been somewhat of a family emergency," Penelope explained evenly.

"O' course, I'll take my leave."

Thinking fast, she took the pile of music and notes to the desk. "Let me just make one more change and you can take these with you."

Picking up a pen, she made a quick note on one of the papers.

My mother is forbidding we speak in fear that we are being improper. But we must finish this book. I will think of a way to work together in secret, for I doubt she'll allow me to visit with Flora for some time.

–Penelope

"There, it's done." Penelope handed him the pile, her note on the last page. "Be sure to look it all over."

"Aye, I will. Good day." He tipped his head at both women before making his exit.

Penelope set her jaw and stalked past her mother, making her way to her bedroom. Thankfully, Cecily didn't follow. As she passed the butler, she ordered him to have the small piano taken up to her chambers. If her mother didn't want her working on the book with Drummond, she would just have to do it behind locked doors.

***

Penelope picked at her dinner, pointedly showing her unhappiness with being forced to abandon her musical pursuits. Her mother kept silent, darting glances at Edmund, willing him to join the fight against Penelope. However, he wasn't one to get involved in 'female matters.'

Once the icy silence became too much, Cecily put down her cutlery and turned toward her husband. "Edmund, dear, isn't it wonderful that Penelope will be going to Hyde Park tomorrow with Theodore Harrison?"

He had a blank look on his face and his mustache twitched beneath his nose. "Who, now?"

"*Theodore. Harrison,*" Cecily hissed.

"The very rich man Mother believes I should marry who owns a lot of boats," Penelope clarified.

"Oh, don't be crude," Cecily said with a heaving sigh.

"Ah, yes." Edmund nodded. "Have fun, darling."

"Edmund, dear," Cecily began again, "wouldn't it be a shame if she did anything to jeopardize her relationship with him?"

Penelope rolled her eyes. "Mother is upset that I have been helping Charlotte's husband's cousin compile a book of songs and stories. She finds it inappropriate."

"Because it is. Isn't it, Edmund?"

He looked between the two women. "Is this really about a book, Cecily?"

"Penelope was entertaining this Scottish gentleman *without* a chaperone."

Edmund's mouth pressed into a thin line. "Penelope, you're old enough to know how unsuitable that is. At your age a lady cannot be alone with a man. I do hope we won't have to have this conversation again."

"Yes, Father," Penelope mumbled, ignoring her mother's pleased expression.

"Pardon me, Miss Elmsly." A footman entered, a small letter on his tray. "A note from Lady MacLeod."

Penelope took the letter and tucked it into the folds of her dress. She assumed that word of her 'family emergency' had reached Charlotte and her old friend was trying to ensure that everything was all right.

No longer having much of an appetite, she excused herself from the table and went up to her room. The footmen had delivered her piano, situating it next to a large window, allowing her some lovely light during the day. She momentarily regretted her decision to give Drummond all of her Scottish notes. The music had grown on her and she was sorry to have seen it go.

She sat down at her desk, where a maid had always kept a lamp lit for her. Using a letter opener, she slipped open the envelope in one movement. When she began reading, she was more than surprised to see what the paper held.

Penelope,

I hope this letter finds you well. I also hope that my presence in your home didn't offend your mother, overly much. I appreciate your passion for this book and do want to push on, if you're still agreeable. I have an idea. If you are willing, leave a light in your window and the latch unlocked tomorrow evening. Send word to Flora if this isn't too forward.

-Drummond by the hand of Flora

P.S.

This is terribly romantic, exciting, and please do agree!

-Flora

Penelope quickly folded the letter up, lest her mother suddenly burst in. Taking a tiny key from one drawer, she hurriedly crouched down. Under her sizeable writing desk was a secret cabinet where she kept all manners of odds and ends. She added Flora's note—or rather, Drummond's—to the small cupboard, locking it up quickly before penning her response.

Flora,

I was sorry to miss you today, but find your proposal of a visit most agreeable. Thank you for returning my hat.

–Penelope

Chapter Nine

"Do remember to sit up straight," Cecily ordered, peering out the window. "And don't talk too much. You know you have a habit of prattling on. And don't run off with him in tow, just let him lead. And if you go for tea, watch you don't stain your dress. And when—"

"Mother, please." Penelope groaned as she fixed the ostrich feathers in her hat.

Cecily turned, her face tight. "Darling, I'm only trying to help."

"You can help by sitting down and having a cup of tea."

"At a time like this?" She appeared scandalized. "I wouldn't dream of it." She crossed the room and took Penelope's hands. "Darling, this is the beginning of the rest of your life."

Penelope slipped out of her mother's grasp just as the butler entered to announce Theodore Harrison's arrival.

"Dear, me!" Cecily snatched a fan from a nearby side table and began fluttering it widely.

"Mrs. Elmsly, Miss Elmsly." Theodore Harrison glided in, holding two bouquets. "How lovely you both look."

"Mister Harrison, it's so nice to see you again," Cecily crooned, pink behind her fan.

"Likewise." He held out a bunch of large, snowy blooms. "These are for you, Madam. The magnolia means nobility, a trait you exude."

Penelope thought her mother might faint from joy as she took the flowers, fanning forgotten. "Goodness! I'll have a maid place these in water straight away."

"And Miss Elmsly," he offered her a bouquet of pale pink blossoms with heavy, fragrant, heads, "please accept these ranunculus. They reminded me, at once, of your charming nature."

"Thank you, Mister Harrison." Penelope smiled, sniffing the petals. "I've never seen these before."

Theodore broke into a grin. "I'm rather a floral enthusiast. I plan on having a moderately sizeable greenhouse when I acquire a country estate."

"A country estate," her mother murmured as a maid came to collect their gifts.

"Shall we be off?" Theodore asked, holding out an arm for Penelope. "Delightful to have seen you again, Mrs. Elmsly."

"The pleasure is mine," Cecily sang.

The butler handed Theodore his hat and Penelope a parasol to ward against the light spring sun. Theodore's two-person cart was stationed outside the Elmsly townhouse, attached to a large dapple-gray.

Theodore helped her up to her seat before letting

himself in and taking the reins. “I thought after a ride through the park, we might see Kensington Gardens, if that would be agreeable?”

“Exceedingly,” Penelope assured, enjoying the feeling of the light breeze as the horse trotted down the lane.

“Do you care for horses, Miss Elmsly?”

“Fine creatures, and I do think you have a rather gorgeous mare.

“Thank you. Horse breeding is a hobby of my brother’s.”

“Do you ride much?”

“When the occasion calls. I enjoy the rogue foxhunt, now and then. Do you?”

Penelope slid her eyes toward Theodore, rather liking the way the sunlight shone on his angular face. “Very much so. But I do enjoy a carriage ride much more.”

Theodore grinned. “Then I’m pleased I suggested it.”

The park came rapidly into view. It was bursting with life. All of society frequently met on the trails. The courting couples weaved between carriages and a stray rowboat glided through the lake. Since it was firmly in the view of many people, it was one of the only places a man and a woman could go together without a dowdy chaperone trailing behind. Penelope knew that to be seen together in the park would solidify their courtship, in a way.

She sat up a bit straighter as people looked their way, feeling a faint gust of pride at being seen with Theodore Harrison. No one would dare speak ill of their courtship, nor would anyone call her an old maid behind their fans. She opened her parasol to keep off the sun. Penelope couldn't risk having browned skin in her wedding dress, after all. She briefly thought of how Theodore would look upon her as she strode gracefully down the aisle on their wedding day, his eyes alight with joy. A perfectly matched pair, they would be the envy of all the guests and Penelope would be confident in her fine choice of a kind and loving husband as she said her vows.

"I've been planning another trip to the west Indies," Theodore told her as the horses trotted along.

"How lovely."

"You like the exotic, am I right?"

"Very much so. I would love to see the Indies. I've heard there are massive elephants and the air is thick with spice."

He nodded, his gaze still on the road. "Yes, they even ride elephants as we ride horses."

"Truly?"

"Yes. I've even ridden one."

Penelope smiled. "I'm so jealous. I've only ever seen one in the zoo and you've seen one up close *and* rode it. What's it like?"

"Like a giant horse with exceedingly wrinkly skin," Theodore told her as he pulled the horses to a stop beneath the shade of several oak trees.

Penelope watched as he tied the reins to a stake beside another pair of bays with an empty cart. The horse pulled toward the grass and began munching happily as Theodore helped her from the cart. He held out his arm and led her to the entrance of

Kensington gardens.

"Please tell me more about your floral interests. Would you say you're quite passionate?" Penelope asked, twirling her parasol a bit with her free hand.

"Yes, I'm extremely interested in botany."

"Is that why you've planned on building your own greenhouse?"

"I find it rather vexing when I'm searching for a particular hothouse flower and the local florists do not have it readily available."

Penelope thought it rather odd that one would go to such lengths for a plant, but chose not to say so. "Then I do hope you'll be able to tell me plenty about the flowers we see today. I must confess, I don't know many facts, just what I think is beautiful."

"It would be my pleasure!" Theodore beamed, patting her hand affectionately.

The pair strolled arm in arm through the gardens. Penelope mainly listened as Theodore told her about each blossom and sometimes she asked a question. He also plucked flowers as they went, and by the time they had reached the carriage, her hands were overflowing.

She pulled a decorative ribbon from her hair and held it out. "Would you mind tying the stems, for me?"

"Certainly." He deftly tied a sturdy bow before helping her into the cart.

When the Elmsly townhouse came into view, she drooped a bit in the carriage's seat. She had found Theodore to be a continuous gentleman and almost wished they could have prolonged their outing.

Still, it would have been improper of them to stay out any longer as the sun was rapidly going down.

"Might I call upon you again?" Theodore asked as he helped her from the jaunting cart.

"I would look forward to it," she replied as they walked up the townhouse stairs.

"Until then." He took her hand, giving it a small kiss in parting.

"Until then."

Penelope had hardly passed her umbrella to the butler when Cecily came flying down the stairs. She was completely out of breath, and barefooted, when she reached the landing.

"Tell me. Everything," she puffed, her hand on the railing.

"Mother, you're going to have a fit." Penelope helped her into the drawing room and sat her down.

"Tell me."

"Goodness, you're persistent."

"I must be when you're so tight-lipped," she snapped. "Now, tell me how it went. What did you speak of? Was he a gentleman? Did many see you on his arm?"

"We spoke of horses and flowers, he was a perfect gentleman, and the park was quite busy. May I retire now?" Penelope asked, already heading to the door.

"Wait, no, tell me more!" Cecily called at her daughter's retreating back.

She ignored her and dashed up the stairs to her room, calling for a candle on her way.

Chapter Ten

Penelope sat in her room, a tall candle in one window just like the letter had instructed. Directly after a hasty dinner, she had withdrawn to her chambers, feigning a headache. The note had not said when she was to expect him, so she was resigned to a lengthy vigil at the glass. She watched the wax slowly drip down the brass holder and pool on the windowsill with no sign of Drummond. The hours crept by at an alarmingly slow rate.

As the grandfather clock struck midnight, Penelope had begun to think he wasn't going to come and it was all a mistake. Perhaps Flora had played a joke on her and merely pretended that the Scotsman was coming to call in the darkness.

The more she reflected on this possibility, the angrier she became. While she didn't believe sweet Flora had it in her to play such a joke, she had the mischievous MacLeod way about her. Charlotte had told her of how playful the siblings were together, always jesting and poking fun. Penelope had looked forward to growing close with Charlotte's new relations, but now she feared they had brought her too far into the fold.

She debated blowing out the candle, but decided on letting it burn. She curled up on her bed, still in her pink silks. Silently stewing, she watched the flame eat the wick, cursing the Scottish idea of humor, until she fell asleep.

***

"Penelope," a voice whispered in her dream. "Penelope."

"Mmm," she responded drowsily.

"Penelope, lass, open your eyes."

She opened her eyelids a sliver to see the large shape of a man cast in shadows, then let out a shrill shriek of alarm only to be rewarded with a hand clamped tightly over her mouth. Beating against the solid chest of her attacker, she fought for escape. She kicked at his body with her slippered feet and felt her heart drop as each kick went unnoticed. It was only when the figure began laughing deep in his chest that she realized who it was.

Arms going slack, she laid still, raising a brow up at him, his features slowly coming together as her eyes adjusted to the darkness.

"It's me, Drummond. Will ye scream if I let ye go?" he asked, fighting more laughter.

Penelope shook her head, allowing him to release her. "Goodness, you certainly know how to treat a lady." She noticed her legs had come uncovered up to the thigh during the struggle and hastily threw her skirts back over them.

"The way ye fought, I thought I had the wrong room."

"The maids and footmen live in the attic rooms, and I live alone with my parents. It would have been them you would have met."

A knock at the door startled them both.

"Go hide in the washroom!" she ordered Drummond in a hiss. Raising her voice, she addressed the knocker. "Who is it?"

"Clara, the maid, Miss Elmsly. I heard you shout out. Are you well?" she asked through the door.

"Yes. I merely saw a nasty spider. Go on to bed, Clara."

As soon as the silence ensured she'd left, Drummond peeked out from behind the washroom door. "A nasty wee spider, am I?"

"A particularly disgusting one." Penelope got off the bed, catching a glimpse of herself in the mirror as she lit a lamp. Most of the pins that held her flaxen hair in place had fallen out in her sleep, leaving a cascade of untidy waves that fell past her shoulders. "Do forgive me. I must look a fright."

Drummond furrowed his brow. "Am I missin' somethin'? Are ye wearin' the wrong color for spring, or whatever it is ye fear?"

She shot him an icy look. "Don't tease. My hair fell down and it's entirely improper."

He chuckled, pulling out the chair to her dressing table and sitting down. "Do no' fash, ye look well enough for bein' scared out o' your wits in the middle o' the night."

"You would be, too, if you were awoken from sleep by a Scotsman holding your mouth shut."

"Ye have quite a set o' lungs on ye."

"I'm flattered you say so," Penelope replied dryly, lighting another lamp. When the room glowed in the warm light, she had to stifle a giggle at the sight before her. The giant Scot, clad in a kilt with a dirk at his hip, looked wildly out of place in her dainty bedchamber among the velvet drapes and delicate dressing accessories. The view was made even more ridiculous when he picked up a vial of perfume and took a sniff, crinkling his nose.

"This smells like horse piss," he grumbled, hastily plugging it back up. "Pardon my language, o' course?"

"Of course." Penelope looked at her windows. Each was shut and not a drape was out of place. "How did you get in?"

"Through the window," he replied, as if it were the obvious answer.

"I would have never known."

"That's the point, is it no'?"

"Well, yes, but how did you get up? It's two stories. Did you use a ladder?" While she had agreed to let him into her room, she hadn't given much thought to how he would scale the walls.

"The stone trimmin' on the sides looks verra pretty, but makes for an easy climb."

"Interesting. Now, shall we begin?" She took a step toward the piano, and then stopped. "Oh, blast it all, I can't use this now. It'll awaken the whole house!"

"Do no' fash, we'll write what we can and ye can do the piano bit later," he said, poking at the odds and ends on the table. "Ye lasses use a verra many potions and powders. It's like ye enjoy playin' witch, or somethin'."

"Drummond, are you always so ridiculously improper?" Penelope scolded, hands upon her hips.

"Only when I'm sneakin' in the window o' a fine lady's bedroom when the rest of the house is abed," he said, his lips twitching with amusement.

Penelope smiled, amused by her own hypocrisy. "You're right, it's hardly proper to fake pretenses when you've done just that."

"And, wouldn't ye know it, I've left the music notes."

"Oh, well, that complicates manners." She removed the vase of ranunculus blossoms and opened her writing desk. "I wish I remembered where we left off."

"Should I run and fetch them?"

"Heavens, no. You were lucky enough to get in here unnoticed once. We shouldn't take unnecessary chances. Just bring them along next time."

"There'll be a next time?"

"How else are we to finish this manuscript?" Penelope asked, pulling out sheets of blank paper and a pen.

"That's mine," Drummond said, pointing at the instrument in her hand. "When ye ran out, ye took it with ye."

She held it out to him. "Oh, I'm sorry."

"Keep it."

"All right, then, move closer so we might keep our voices low," she ordered, making room for a second chair at the desk.

Drummond relocated the dressing table's stool next to her, his arm brushing hers as he sat. His sleeves were bared to the elbow and the heat radiated off him in waves. He was so near, Penelope could smell him—the scent of wood smoke, sweet whiskey, and hay greeted her. She blushed, focusing on the paper before her to control her odd thoughts. It wasn't her business what he smelled like.

"Nice flowers," he said, motioning toward Theodore's blooms.

"Oh, thank you."

"From a gentleman caller, aye?"

"Yes, they are." She watched his jaw set from the corner of her eye.

"Would it be the fop ye went for a carriage ride with, today?" he asked, a dark shadow marring his features.

Penelope shot her gaze toward him. "He's not a fop. Mister Harrison is very polite and owns a shipping business. Wait, I didn't see you in the park today."

"Because I was no' there. Some new friend of Flora's came for tea and told us all ye had a beau."

"He's not my beau. We merely took a ride to see the blooms." She heaved a sigh. "Why am I even explaining myself to you?"

He shrugged crossing his arms over his massive chest. "We're just havin' a chat."

"Chat, indeed. Now, can we get something done before the night is entirely over?"

The two worked until the early pink light began to seep in though the edges of the drapery. Penelope was rather glad that the night was nearly over. Her eyes were heavy with fatigue and her penmanship was suffering greatly. Several legends and stories had been written down, their heads close together as they whispered in the light of the lamps. But still, Penelope longed to get out of her stays and into her bed.

"It's going to be morning, soon," Drummond said, looking over toward the window. "I must away before anyone's awake to see me."

"Will you be all right getting back down?"

"Aye." He stood, stretching. "Same time tomorrow?"

"Tomorrow?"

"Unless ye'd like to wait?" he asked as he threw open the shades and began to wedge the windowpane upward.

"Oh, of course not. We need to finish this soon before you leave to go back to Scotland." She rose from her seat and stood by the wall next to Drummond. She wanted to see how he made it safely to the ground below.

"We will no' leave so soon as to let this book go unfinished."

"Then I'll see you tomorrow night?" The thought heartened her and began to make her think fondly of the next sleepless night before she pushed the feeling down, attempting to ignore her pleasure.

"Tomorrow night," he promised, stepping out of the window and giving her one last glance of his pearly teeth.

Penelope leaned out into the night, her hair whipping around her face as she watched Drummond leap from the thick sill to a short outcropping. Noiselessly, his feet hit the stone outside the house with cat-like grace. He looked from one side to the other before turning his face back up toward her window. He held up a hand, giving her a brief wave.

She wiggled her fingers at him, smiling at the thrill of getting away with both sneaking a man in and out of her room without anyone noticing. Then there was their casual interaction. Penelope had never acted so with a man. Of course, with Charlotte she sat about with her hair down and talked of ideas and fancies, but doing so with Drummond seemed almost too natural.

Once the window was latched, her gown put away, and her corset abandoned on the floor, Penelope finally slid beneath her sheets and nestled into her down pillow. She drifted off to sleep feeling accomplished, fulfilled, and with the smell of wood smoke in her nose.

Chapter Eleven

The next evening, she waited by the open window eagerly, her fingers tapping upon the sill in impatience. Penelope prepared for his visit by ensuring she was properly dressed and not asleep like a slovenly maid with her hair unbound. She'd even gone down to the kitchen to gather a few refreshments, meats, cheese, bread, some teacakes, and a pitcher of freshly pressed lemonade to share.

Just as the clock's hands crept toward midnight, she saw Drummond strolling casually down the road, a bag in hand. As he passed under each lamppost, his massive size cast a shadow, and when he stopped in front of her house, he looked up at her. In the darkness, the white flash of a toothy grin was all she could see as he began his ascent.

"Good o' ye to no' be sleepin' this night," Drummond said as he closed her bedroom window.

"Well, lovely evening to you, as well," Penelope retorted, fetching her tray of treats. "I brought these up to snack on."

"Did ye make them yourself?" he asked, taking a

teacake.

Penelope found herself flushing. “Oh, no, I don’t know how to cook.”

“Well, then, my compliments to your cook. This is a fine cake.” Drummond polished it off and handed her the satchel.

“Oh, I see you remembered the notes.” She eagerly slipped them from the bag and took them to her writing desk. “I’ll just match these up with their accompanying stories.”

As he did the night before, Drummond slid the stool from her dressing table and sat beside her, watching her flip through the papers. “Ye kept your hair up tonight.”

“Obviously,” she answered, her focus glued to the sheet music. “Last night my pins fell out as I slept. I would have never taken my hair down on purpose.”

“No, the pins no’ bother ye? I thought it would be more comfortable to leave them out.”

The pins, which she had ignored up until this point, *were* beginning to pinch her scalp. “It can pain me at times, but one must get used to such discomforts in order to keep propriety.”

“It’s only me here. Surely, ye can forgo the pins in my company.”

Her gaze flitted up to his. “*Surely*, I cannot. You’re a man, I’m a lady, and we’re being improper as it is.”

Straight-faced, he reached up and deftly plucked a pin from her curls, releasing a single blonde tendril.

“Drummond!” Penelope hissed, snatching at the

pin as he held it beyond her reach. "That was horrid of you."

"Was it?" he asked, pulling another one free and tossing it to the floor.

"I'm serious, stop it."

"I do no' think I will."

Penelope felt another pin release its grasp and she huffed in irritation. Although, she did admit that the relief her head felt was easing her annoyance, but only slightly. "Now I probably look ridiculous. Give me the pins back."

His emerald eyes flashed and his lips pulled into an amused smile. "No one is here to witness the scandal, save me." He removed the last pins. "That's better then, aye?"

"Well, yes," she confessed. "But, don't think you can take such liberties in the future."

"Do no' fash, we'll be the picture of respectability when in public."

Penelope turned back to the pages at hand. "Now that you're done being a pest, we can get some work done."

As she paired up papers and made herself notes in the margins, she could feel his gaze upon her. The customary feeling of being exposed before him hit her once again, and Penelope attempted to focus her thoughts purely on the music. But as she sensed Drummond's closeness and the particular way he considered her every movement, she found it harder to concentrate.

"Can't you find something productive to do?" she asked, her cheeks hot.

"I am doin' somethin' mighty productive." His

voice was low and he breached the space between them. "I'm learnin' every strand o' hair and the faint curve o' your cheek. I'm learnin' the way your lashes look in the lamplight and the way ye blush when ye know I'm watchin' ye, but dare not look back. I think puttin' to memory every inch o' your face is the most productive thing I've done in a good while."

Penelope felt her heart race in her chest, straining against her tight corset. The sound echoed in her ears and her eyes stayed fastened to the pen in her hand. She couldn't even bring herself to look at him, although his face was so close, she could feel his breath upon her arm. What he said was common, disrespectful, and so beautiful she thought her beating heart might break.

Drummond reached out, tucking a curl behind her ear, his fingers lingering. "Did I overstep?"

"You know you did," she whispered.

"I'm sorry." He took his hand away. "Are ye angry with me?"

She felt coldness in the space on her neck where his touch had been. A deep part of her wished that he would touch her again. "You know that I am." But she could not allow such familiar closeness.

"Then I'll take my leave. I'm sorry, I did no' mean to be so, I just could no' help myself. I could no' keep those words in any longer." He sounded sad now, and stood from his seat, preparing to make his descent down to the lane below.

"Wait!" Penelope called out, louder than she should have. "Don't go."

"I do no' want to give attention where it is no'

wanted."

She stood tentatively, watching the slow rise and fall of his back as he looked out the window. "But I *do* want it, even though I know I should not."

He turned back to her, swallowing hard. Drummond swiftly pulled Penelope to him, holding her closer than she had ever been held by a man. His large hands were at her waist and she was pressed against his enormous chest, hearing each thump of his heart as it matched her own. The nearness tightened her throat and she breathed in his intoxicating scent. She had never been to Scotland, but in his arms, she could imagine what it might be like.

Drummond drew back, gazing down at her. "Penelope, I know we do no' know each other verra well, but I have to confess, when I saw ye had those flowers from another man, I could no' help but feel seething jealousy. I had to tell ye what I thought, even if it was no' a good idea."

"You're so poetic."

He laughed. "Ye sound surprised."

Penelope looked up sheepishly. "If we're both making confessions, I have to say, when I met you, I thought you nothing more than a very big guardsman with nothing to say. But you're so much more than that. It frightens me."

"I do no' mean to frighten ye."

"No, it's not *you.* It's the feelings you stir within me and the beautiful words you speak. The newness of it is almost horrifying."

He brushed a hand against her face, leaving streaks of delicious heat in its path. "Then I'll say those things a thousand times until they no longer scare ye. I do no' know what to make o' this, either, but we'll learn together, aye?"

Penelope nodded and Drummond leaned closer, tentatively lifting her chin upward. Bending down slightly, he placed a careful kiss upon her lips. His gentleness surprised her. He handled her like a sparrow and touched her ever so lightly, as if he feared she might break. She stood on her toes, pushing for more. A primal hunger stirred within her and she reached up, placing both arms around his neck.

His hand slid into her hair, pulling her face nearer as his kiss deepened. His other hand had a vice-like grip on her hip and she could feel each finger imprinting into her side. Penelope still found herself craving to be even more connected. Her breasts thrust against his muscular chest with each labored breath as she fumbled though the new motions of intimacy.

Drummond was the one who finally broke the embrace, with one last caress of his lips. "I can no' continue. I'm no' a strong enough man."

"A strong enough man?" Penelope panted as she slid her hands down his strong shoulders and clung to his shirt. Her hunger hadn't been sated and she found she was positively ravenous.

"I can no' resist ye. Ye do somethin' to me I can no' explain." His palm drifted the length of her corset and back up, just beneath her breast. "I can no' control myself."

"Just kiss me once again." Penelope surprised herself with the boldness that escaped her lips.

While she had been internally begging for more, she would never have imagined herself actually imploring him for another embrace.

Drummond groaned, his face tightening with effort. Gently, he leaned in, brushing her lips with his. "Just one. Tis all I can manage." He pulled away then, smiling down at her from his full height. "Now, I must go."

"Go?" Penelope repeated, her face turned up toward his, almost two feet above her own. She clutched tightly to his arm, remembering its beautiful heat without the covering of a shirt. She longed to feel it again. "But it's not morning yet."

"If I stay, we might do somethin' we'll both regret," he said remorsefully.

Penelope agreed with him, but could only manage a slight nod. She cleared her throat and tried to disregard the queer burning in her core. Where she once felt odd in his searing gaze, she now relished the heat in abundance.

Drummond opened the window, throwing one leg over the ledge. With one final glance in her direction, he disappeared back into the night, leaving Penelope alone.

Chapter Twelve

Penelope and her parents arrived at Charlotte's new orphanage precisely at noon. The corner building, once a sewing factory, now featured a sign that read ***'MacLeod Home for Youths'*** in gilded letters. A group of spectators crowded around the front steps where a beaming Charlotte stood, her husband close at hand. The women waved at one another over the heads of the guests and Penelope left her parents to venture closer to the steps.

As she weaved through the thick crowd, her eyes met Drummond's. He was standing near the front doors, his height making him easily visible. Penelope felt heat creep up her neck and pool in her cheeks as he gave her a familiar nod and small, jovial smirk. Memories of stealthy caresses from the night before washed over her in waves. She was about to go to him when she heard her name from behind her.

"Miss Elmsly, I hoped to find you here." Theodore Harrison tipped his hat at her, a smile on his classically handsome face. "Will you allow me the honor of escorting you this afternoon?"

Penelope cast an embarrassed look in Drummond's direction only to find that the space he once occupied was empty. "That would be delightful, thank you," she replied, taking Theodore's arm.

Flora had been hidden in the masses, and now stepped forward. "Penelope, lovely to see you."

"Flora, do you know Mister Theodore Harrison?" Penelope asked.

"Yes, we were acquainted at your birthday ball," Theodore said, nodding in greeting.

"Penelope, how *is* that book you're working on coming along?" Flora's expression was placid, but her dark blue eyes gleamed mischievously.

Penelope cleared her throat. "Oh, well, it's coming together nicely, thank you."

"A book?" Theodore sounded surprised. "Why, I had no idea you were working on such a project."

"Oops!" Flora faked embarrassment and let out a strange sounding chuckle. "Dear, me. I plum forgot that Penelope was keeping her work a secret. How terrible of me."

"Well, I'd like to read it."

"I, as well," Flora agreed. "I've heard it's positively *titillating*."

Penelope was saved by the sound of Charlotte ringing a bell, signaling her commencement. Thankfully, Theodore and Flora were focused on the stairs, and she allowed herself to take a deep breath.

"Good afternoon, and thank you for joining me on this exciting day." Charlotte's voice was clear and steady. “Giving a home, food, and education to the orphans of London has always been dear to my heart. After seeing how wonderfully the parentless children of Scotland were treated, I knew that a change was needed here. As of today, we are capable of taking in thirty children and plan on further expansion in the fall. But we need the help of gracious benefactors to keep these children adequately cared for. Now, I’d like to invite you all inside for some refreshment and to take a tour of our facilities.”

The crowd clapped politely and Penelope suppressed the desire to cheer. She wondered when her friend became such a refined lady capable of holding a rapt audience. Charlotte had certainly grown in the year since meeting Conner, and Penelope loved him for it.

“Dashing notion,” Theodore stated, reaching into his coat pocket and pulling out his checkbook. “Very noble.”

“Charlotte’s always had a soft spot for children.”

“As do I.” He scribbled an amount on the draft and ended it with a twirling signature. “Miss Elmsly, would you be so kind as to make my introduction to Lady MacLeod?”

“Of course.” Penelope excused them from Flora’s company and joined the line to greet Charlotte and Conner. “Do you have many philanthropic pursuits, Mister Harrison?”

“When I see a cause in need, I enjoy sharing my wealth. I have an abundance and it’s only right that I help when necessary.”

“That’s very kind of you.” Penelope meant it.

Most of the wealthy she knew kept tight holds on their purses.

"Penelope, I'm so glad you could come." Charlotte embraced her as they neared the entrance while Conner introduced himself to Theodore. "Did you come together?" she asked in a whisper.

"No, we just met here. I didn't know he was even coming…"

"Lady MacLeod," Theodore said, handing Charlotte the check, "please accept this donation for the children."

Penelope saw the number on the paper and nearly fainted. Theodore was contributing one thousand pounds to the orphanage. While Charlotte had the tact to merely thank him and tuck the note away without reading it, Penelope fought to control her excitement for her friend. She knew Theodore might have only been showing off for her benefit, but it pleased her all the same.

"I'll see you soon." Charlotte smiled at the pair, ushering them forward to accept the next visitors.

Once they were in the new, tastefully furnished entryway, Theodore turned to her. "May I get you something to drink?"

"Thank you, that would be lovely."

"I'll return in a moment." Smiling, he pressed his lips to the back of her hand in a gentleman's farewell.

Penelope stood alone in the moderately sized hall, watching the visitors mingle on the main floor. She hoped that all of them were just as generous with their donations. Theodore's charity was endearing and the way he spoke of spreading his abundant wealth heartened her. The more she reflected, the more she wondered what kind of man he was when he wasn't trying to impress. Or maybe he really was just a philanthropist who chose to share his wealth with those in need. Penelope suspected that his kind heart—

"Come with me," a man's voice growled in her ear before he pulled her into a closed-off room, slamming the door behind them.

Penelope spun to find her assaulter. "Drummond, what is the meaning of this?"

His size appeared more imposing due to the rage in his eyes. For a moment, Penelope was almost frightened, but she knew enough to not be truly scared. "Ye know what this is about, ye wee vixen."

"Vixen?" Penelope gasped. "Are you mad? You're the one acting like a beast!"

He laughed from deep in his chest. "Me, a beast? I'll show ye what a beast I can be."

Drummond seized her by the waist, making her drop her fan to the floor. Roughly, he smashed his lips against hers, manipulating her with his mouth. Penelope was too stunned to move at first, but soon found she eased into his movements instinctually, one hand clasping his bulging bicep, another clutching his shoulder to steady herself as her knees grew weak.

Penelope felt his hand drift from her waist, up to her chest, grazing her breast with his palm. She gasped into his mouth in both shock and exhilaration. The sound of her gentle mewling only built his fire and he dragged his mouth down her neck, nipping as he went. Panting, she clutched his thick russet hair and nearly let out a cry when she felt a small bite at her collarbone. She heard him moan as he kneaded her breast, his breath hot upon her neck.

Slowly, he moved his fingers up to her face, cupping her cheeks as his kisses lessened in ferocity to gentle strokes of lips and tongue. Penelope's legs were trembling with passion and she was grateful she had a strong arm to keep her upright. She nearly fell to the ground when he released her. The only thing holding her up was her hand, steadying herself upon a wall.

"I do no' want to see another man kiss ye," he rumbled, his eyes a stormy sea of rage. "Ever."

Penelope watched as he left the room, so dazed she could barely think straight. Her lips were swollen from their embrace and she felt a carnal heat in her loins as she tried to catch her breath. Their kiss the night before had been demanding and sensual but this series of caresses was almost primitive in nature, and gave her a peculiar stirring feeling she couldn't quite place. Or maybe she was simply afraid to place it.

As she caught her breath, she straightened her dress, her bodice shifted from Drummond's groping and her hair mussed. Penelope had almost no concept of time and wondered how long she had been here. There was no mirror to be found in the small, empty room, so she had to take a chance that her appearance was decent.

"Oh, Miss Elmsly, there you are." Theodore was outside the door when she entered the hall, a drink in either hand. "Are you all right? You look rather flushed."

Penelope patted her bouffant, trying to look calm and unaffected. "Oh, I merely saw a spider."

"Dreadful creatures," he consoled, giving her a glass of spring cider.

"Terrible," she agreed as she sipped the cool beverage, hoping it would lessen the rosiness of her cheeks. She briefly wished she still had her fan, but didn't want to bring up the fact that she had lost it during a romp with Drummond.

Together, the finely matched pair meandered through the new orphanage, tittering about the restored architecture and the recently unpacked schoolroom. Penelope browsed the crowd as they walked, half hoping, half not, to see Drummond again. But as the sun began to set and Theodore delivered her back to her parents, she knew he was gone.

***

When the Elmsly family returned to their townhouse, Penelope could barely stand to eat her dinner. She excused herself early and soaked in a bath, hoping the warm waters would relax her. Mixed emotions were churning in her stomach—her blasphemous longing for Drummond, her polite fondness for dear Theodore Harrison, societal rules she knowingly broke, and her own wonton behavior.

After she redressed in a clean nightgown, Penelope almost lit a new candle to place in the window for Drummond. But as she pulled the tinder box from her nightstand, she paused, thinking back to how dreadfully angry he had been with her. There was a wrath seething within him that Penelope imagined must've been the same lethal look he had upon the battlefield.

She felt, deep within her, that Drummond wouldn't be visiting her that night.

Shivering, she put away the candle and tinder and crawled into bed. She listened to the faint rain that had begun to fall, pelting the windows and dripping through the leaves of the elm beside her bedroom. While Penelope felt a pang of disappointment that she would be spending the night actually *sleeping*, she was grateful for the chance to have some moments alone and for not having to face Drummond. She fell asleep to the tinkling of the rain, wondering what tomorrow might hold.

***

When she felt a gentle graze upon her cheek like a wisp of silk, Penelope drifted out of a deep slumber. The sensation was warm and familiar in a strange way. The dream seemed so real and comforting. But soon she realized she was fully awake, and she found herself looking into a pair of illuminated cat-eyes that stared back through pure darkness.

"Drummond?" she asked, groggy, unsure if she was really awake.

"Aye." He was crouched beside her bed, his face level with hers. His hair was damp with rain, but he didn't seem bothered by it.

Slowly, she sat up, still trying to fully rouse herself. "What are you doing here?"

"I thought ye would be expectin' me, but I see I was mistaken."

"I'm sorry. I didn't put a candle out because I thought you were cross with me."

"Cross with ye?" He frowned, pushing the damp tendrils away from his face before sitting on the edge of the bed by her knees.

"Well, you seemed rather angry at the orphanage opening. I really thought you wouldn't want to come tonight." She squinted. He moved farther away, making it difficult to see more than his shadowy form. "Goodness, it's certainly a dark night."

"Aye, there's no moon, and even if there was, the storm would have hidden it."

Penelope reached into her drawer and pulled out a candle, igniting it swiftly and smiling when the dim glow illuminated them. "That's better. As I was saying, I didn't think you'd come."

"I'd never pass up a chance to see ye, even if ye have a simperin' fop at your heels."

"Jealousy doesn't become you," Penelope chastised half-heartedly. His admission of possessiveness secretly pleased her and filled her with liquid fire that began to course through her veins up to her cheeks.

"Aye, perhaps no'. But, I have to say, ye in a nightdress with your hair loose about ye, does suit ye greatly."

Penelope gasped, drawing the blankets up,

covering her bared shoulders and body beneath the thin shift. "Goodness, Drummond! I'm barely dressed. Fetch my robe. This is entirely inappropriate!"

"Ye are always preoccupied with what is proper when ye invite a man to your bedchambers in the wee hours o' the night," he said, taking off his boots to muffle the sounds of his movements.

"I'm aware of the hypocrisy, but that doesn't lessen the seriousness of my demands."

"Ach, do no' fash," he said, crossing the room to her wardrobe where her wrap hung upon the door. "I'll get it for ye."

"Good, now pass it to me quickly."

He held up her silk robe, a good ten paces away from the bed. "I've taken it halfway. Ye come the rest." His voice was serious, but Penelope could see the way his eyes flashed with mischief. She wondered if all Scottish people were constantly filled with unbridled mirth at every moment.

"You know that I can't." Penelope felt heat rise up from her chest, both from anger and a perplexing feeling of excitement that tickled her stomach and the tops of her thighs.

"Do your legs no' work?" he teased, dangling her prize before her.

She huffed. "Fine. Close your eyes."

He knitted his brows. "Ye jest with me?"

"No. Close your eyes, Drummond MacGregor."

When she was sure he obeyed, she slipped from bed and crossed the room carefully to reclaim her wrap. As soon as her fingers brushed the silk, Drummond's hand snapped out, snatching her by the waist and drawing her in. His damp shirt was plastered to his skin, transferring the rain to her thin nightdress. He then pressed his lips against hers, catching her fully by surprise.

"Drummond!" She gasped into his mouth, feeling her nipples harden between the two thin layers of cloth that separated them.

He silenced her with another kiss, harder this time, with an urgency that was mutually felt. Driven by desire, she reached up, tangling her fingers in his hair. She heard a pleasurable rumble within his chest as he begged for entrance into her mouth with his tongue. Penelope had never been kissed in such a way. No man, before Drummond, had ever kissed her. But she found the new sensation of intertwined limbs and panting breaths exceedingly agreeable.

As the wetness from Drummond's walk to the Elmsly townhouse shifted to her nightgown, Penelope shivered, the growing fire from their passion doing little to warm the dampness from the early spring showers.

"Are ye cold?" he whispered, nipping at her neck.

"A little," she admitted between ragged breaths.

Keeping a hand at her hip, he pulled his wet shirt from his chest and tossed it to the ground. He glanced down appraisingly. She knew he could see her full breasts rise and fall through the wide neck of her shift. The nightgown was now translucent from the water and stuck to Penelope's pale skin.

"We must get this frock off ye," Drummond said, his gaze still glued to her chest and his voice low with lust. "Ye'll catch your death if ye keep it on."

His husky words created a new wetness between Penelope's legs and she suddenly felt all thoughts of propriety and decency leave her. She nimbly untied the ribbon that held the neck of her nightdress closed. The neck widened and slipped over her shoulders, pooling at the ground beneath her feet. Penelope heard Drummond take a sharp intake of breath.

He muttered something in guttural Scottish before pulling her to him again and half-carrying her to bed. His mouth found hers as he lay beside her, his hands skimming her slim stomach and hips. Goosebumps rose upon her flesh and she eagerly leaned into the heat radiating from his muscular body. Uncertainly, she placed a hand upon his stone chest, feeling the rapid beating of his warrior heart beneath her palm.

"Do ye feel what ye do to me?" Drummond asked, covering her hand with his. "Your touch makes my heart pound firmer and stouter than anythin' else in this world."

"I hardly understand this, what's happening between us, but I find that I can't help myself," Penelope confessed, her gaze trapped in his emerald ones.

"Then don't. Enjoy this moment with me and let yourself go."

Their lips crashed together as Drummond explored her body in a deliciously slow manner. He took his time as his hands dipped between her breasts, traveled down her navel, and swept the expanse of her backside, gripping the supple flesh, making Penelope moan. Her sounds of pleasure grew as Drummond's mouth followed, settling upon her breast, sucking one nipple. She thrust her hips toward him, meeting with a firm object pressing against her mound.

"Drummond," she gasped, holding his head to her breast, "your dirk is pressing into me."

"I did no' wear my weapon tonight." He smirked, rising up to take her mouth again.

Penelope reached down to touch the offending hardness, finding it attached to his body beneath his kilt. She knew at once what it was and snatched her hand away, embarrassed with her naivety.

"It will no' bite ye," Drummond laughed. "But I will." He nipped at her collarbone.

Penelope longed for more—more of what, she couldn't say. But, she found herself even hungrier for the unknown when she felt him touch her at the coppice between her thighs. He gently stroked the tender flesh, making her whimper with new desire. She pushed her hips into his hand, allowing him greater access.

Drummond made a strangled sound deep within his throat. "Penelope, you're so wet, so soft."

"More," she murmured, curving into his palm. "I need more."

"Then I will deliver it."

Penelope muffled a small cry as she felt something enter her, the strange sensation replaced with one of bliss as he continued his manipulations. His fingers, skilled with a bow and sword, were equally accomplished when he touched her. Penelope grasped his shoulders as she felt waves of unimaginable ecstasy wash over her. Her nails dug into his shoulder and she placed the other to her mouth, trying to control her sighs of pleasure.

When the stirring within her was momentarily sated, Penelope felt a sense of shame fill its place. Looking up into Drummond's grinning face, she felt a disgraceful heat pool in her cheeks. She bit her lip and turned her gaze away. She wasn't sure what had happened between them, but she knew it was immoral and improper.

"Penelope." His voice was low with worry. "Are ye all right?"

Her lower lip trembled. "Yes, I'm fine."

"Do no' lie to me." He pulled the blanket over her and laid a hand on her arm. "What's wrong?"

"We just…I…" The tears of humiliation rolled down her cheeks.

"Ach, do no' cry." Drummond brushed a hand through his hair. "Did I scare ye? Do somethin' ye did no' want?"

"Oh, it's not that. Well, it *is*. Don't you see?" She faced him again, staring, not into his eyes, but at the soft space where his neck met his shoulder, watching his pulse slow. "I *did* want it. I wanted it so much."

He brushed his knuckles against her cheek. "Then what's wrong?"

"I shouldn't have wanted it as much as I did. I let you look upon my nakedness and touch my most secret places. And I *enjoyed* it."

"Then you're ashamed? You're ashamed ye let me touch ye." He withdrew his hand and rolled onto his back, sighing at the ceiling. "I'm sorry, I did no' think I would disgust ye so." He rubbed at the scar etched upon his chest and began to move. "I'll take my leave now. And will no' bother ye again."

Penelope grabbed his arm as he stood. "No, please."

"Penel—Miss Elmsly, it's all right," he said in a soft voice. "I'm a grown man. Ye do no' need to cater to my emotions."

"No, you're misunderstanding me. Please just wait." She sat up, clutching the coverlet to her chest. "Please don't go. I'm not ashamed of you, I never would be. I'm ashamed of baring myself and revealing my body to a man I am not married to. And the most appalling part of all is that I *enjoyed* it. I relished the feelings you gave me, although I feel immoral."

His jaw set as he surveyed her, but his face relaxed with every passing moment. "When I see ye like this, bathed in moonlight with your fair hair about your shoulders and ye lookin' up at me with those eyes, I can no' think o' anywhere else I'd rather be." Drummond sat beside her, folding her into his arms. "What's happened between us, and whatever will, is only between us. No one ever need know. I would never shame ye, Penelope."

"Will you stay with me? Just for a while?" she asked, nestling into his shoulder and feeling safer with every passing moment. The sound of his heart and the scent of his skin was almost intoxicating

"I would like that verra much."

Penelope allowed him to soothe her. She melted in his hold, breathing in his now familiar scent as they lay together in her four-poster bed, in her family home, on the fashionable side of London. She knew he would never betray her confidence, nor brag about his conquest, but the feelings of shame still lingered in her core. But even more than shame, she felt fulfilled, as if she was finally complete.

Chapter Thirteen

"Miss Elmsly, have you awakened?" A maid knocked upon Penelope's bedroom door, a rapid series of swift sounds.

Penelope, still half asleep called out, "Yes, you may come in."

"No, they can no'…" Drummond's hushed voice said into her ear.

Her eyes shot open, startled at her sudden awareness of his presence. "Drummond, what—"

"Get rid o' the maid."

Penelope cleared her voice. "Actually, I'd like to stay in bed a while longer!" she called out. "I'll dress myself!"

Drummond slipped from the bed and Penelope was scandalized to see his naked buttocks heading toward the door. She heard the click of the lock. When he turned to return to her, she covered her eyes with her bare arm.

"Oh, sorry," he mumbled. "A Scot never sleeps in his plaid."

"Put something on, for goodness sake!"

Penelope hissed, glad she had the foresight to don her own nightdress before falling asleep.

He kissed her shoulder, bared by the wide neck of her gown. “As ye wish.”

“What are we going to do?” Penelope asked, her gaze trained on the wall opposite Drummond as he dressed.

“Do no’ fear, it’ll be fine.”

She huffed, trying to ignore the swelling pang of nausea as she envisioned her parents dying of shame and horror at finding them together. “How? It’s already morning. Are you planning on just strolling down the stairs and having a bit of tea with my father on the way out?”

“Ye can open your eyes now. I’m decent.”

Penelope slid her gaze toward Drummond to see him sitting at her dressing table, pulling on his boots. “We’re in so much trouble.”

“Do no’ fash, *leannan,* sneakin’ in and out o’ places is a Highland specialty.” He winked at her and stood, twitching the curtains open to peer outside. “It’s still early enough that there are no’ many people on the road.”

“*Leannan*?” Penelope mimicked. She was about to ask what it meant when she remembered how dire their situation was. “All right then, Highlander, get out before someone catches you.”

“What? Ye do no’ want your father to catch us abed and force us to marry?” He threw a hand to his heart. “Ye wound me.”

“Enough jokes. You have to leave.”

He crossed the room and kissed her softly on the forehead. “I’ll send word if I’m caught by the authorities."

"Don't jest, just go," she hissed sternly, pushing him toward the window with one hand, only allowing him to pause to grab his shirt from the floor and pull it over his head.

As soon as he disappeared over the ledge, Penelope crept to the drapery. She looked down to the lane finding it gloriously empty. Pleased at how quickly he disappeared, she found her dressing robe and tied it tightly around her waist. She caught a glimpse of herself in the mirror and appraised her refection in a new light. With white blonde hair and clear eyes, she had always been a beauty. But, now with cheeks red from Drummond's touch and lips that were full from a night of passion, she would call herself truly beautiful.

She was just about to pull herself away from the dressing table and dress for breakfast when there was a knock at the door.

"Miss Elmsly, Lady MacLeod is here for you," a maid called through the door. "Your mother has sent her up."

Eagerly, Penelope rushed to the door and unlocked it. "Charlotte, please come in!" She glanced at the maid. "Bring up some refreshment."

Once the door was shut behind them, Charlotte immediately turned on her friend. "Penelope Elmsly, why was there a large Scotsman creeping from your bedroom window as I came down the lane, just now?"

Penelope paled, but quickly composed herself. "Whatever do you mean? I've been asleep until right this very moment."

“Is that so?” Charlotte scanned the room, her gaze focusing on something just under the edge of the ruffled bed skirt. “Then what’s that?”

“What’s what?” Penelope asked. She knew Drummond hadn’t brought anything but the clothes on his back, and left in the very same set.

Charlotte went to the bed and plucked something off the floor, pausing to glance at it before showing it to Penelope, a smirk upon her lips. “How peculiar. I saw a certain Scotsman scaling the walls of your townhouse, and now I find a Scottish pin on the floor in your room.”

The silver pin sported a lion wearing a crown, enclosed within a circle that sported a Gaelic phrase. “This could be anyone’s,” Penelope said.

“But it’s a *MacGregor* crest on a pin commonly worn by *Drummond* MacGregor.” Charlotte handed the pin to Penelope. “What’s going on? I saw you at the opening with Theodore Harrison.”

“I didn’t go with him, he was just there and offered to escort me.”

“Then what’s going on with Drum?”

“Nothing!” Penelope grimaced, fingering the crest. “Well, almost nothing. I don’t know.”

“Penelope, are you still…a maid?”

She blushed a deep red, holding the neck of her robe closed. “Yes, but barely.”

Charlotte grinned. “You little vixen!”

“Why do you sound so pleased?”

“Because I am!” She grasped Penelope’s hands. “Don’t you see? This is fantastic. When we leave for Scotland, you can follow us!”

“Wait, no, it’s not like that.”

Charlotte released her excited hold. “Then, what is it?”

“We’re not in love, or getting married, or anything of the sort. We merely fell into…lust together.”

“You know that’s how things started between Conner and I,” she pointed out.

Penelope sighed, holding tight to the pin. “I just don’t know. He makes me feel so, unexplainably strange. It’s like he knows what I’m thinking and what I need.”

“And it scares you?”

“It does.”

“Do you want to go to him now? We can tell your parents we are going to the shops.”

Penelope bit her lip. “I do, but I shouldn’t.”

“Why not?”

“I just need some distance to think.”

“You could come with us, you know,” Charlotte said quietly. “And you would be happy in Scotland.”

“Or I could be happy in England.”

“Come to dinner tonight, yes? Now that the orphanage is open, we have to leave as soon as we have our things packed. Conner will leave on the morrow, if he’s given the chance.”

Penelope’s face fell. “No, you can’t leave!”

“We’ve been away for so long. Between the wedding, the honeymoon, and waiting for the orphanage, it’s been a few months.”

“What time shall I come to dinner, then?”

***

Penelope took extra care in dressing that evening, selecting a pale blue chiffon gown with pale pink rosettes tucked within the folds. She slipped Drummond's crest into her small, beaded purse. Taking one last look in her dressing mirror, she called for a carriage.

She felt rather odd about going to dinner while knowing that Charlotte was privy to her indiscretions. While Charlotte had sworn herself to secrecy, Penelope wasn't sure if her dearest friend could keep her mouth closed around her husband. Surely Conner would be more than pleased to hear that Penelope and his cousin were getting along so swimmingly. But Penelope needed to pretend every MacLeod in London didn't know about her midnight liaisons.

When she arrived at the MacLeod home, Penelope attempted to stay calm. As long as she maintained a composed demeanor, certainly no one would suspect she was involved in any form of impropriety. But as she tried to take on a collected appearance, her mind kept drifting to the surreptitious caresses of the night before. She was sure her discomfiture was fully apparent by the flush she felt climb up her neck.

"Penelope!" Flora smiled, peering down at her from the landing at the top of the stairs. "I'm so pleased you could come! Charlotte said you were staying overnight."

"I am. The footmen are delivering my things. That green gown is positively darling on you."

Flora tore down the steps, embracing Penelope. "And your dress is perfect. I do love you in blue."

Penelope hooked her arm through Flora's and the pair began their walk into the drawing room. "Is there a large group this evening? Charlotte didn't say."

"No, it's just us."

"Miss Elmsly." Conner gave Penelope a theatrical bow as she entered.

"Ignore him, he's merely celebrating the return to Scotland," Charlotte explained, obviously unimpressed by her husband's dramatics.

"Penelope." Drummond gave her a short nod from his usual place by the fire. His eyes smoldered and she felt the heat burn her skin.

Flora appraised them knowingly, and squeezed her arm. "I'll let you two catch up. I know it's been *ages* since you have spoken."

Penelope glared at the little Scottish woman as she waltzed over to the bookcase to inspect a novel. She crept toward Drummond, who grinned as she neared. Penelope ignored the itching in her hands that longed to touch his handsome face, or the bared skin of his arm.

"Ye look lovely in blue," he said, considering her with a cautious gaze. "I'm glad to see ye."

"And I, you." She rifled in her purse and withdrew the crested pin. "I believe this is yours?"

He smirked, looking at the little piece of metal. "Aye, I wondered where I left it. Your bed was goin' to be the first place I looked."

Penelope slapped his arm with her bag. "Shut your mouth, Drummond MacGregor."

"If I do no', will ye shut it for me?"

"You're incorrigible. Just take the pin and you

needn't worry about your mouth. "

"How about I get it from ye later?" he asked, folding her fingers around the pin.

"Pretend to be proper, just a tad, while we're at dinner," Penelope ordered, putting the crest back into her purse and snapping the clasp shut.

"And then after dinner?" he asked suggestively, his hand grazing the side of her arm.

Penelope felt the hairs on the back her neck stand up. "After dinner come drinks."

"I'll get ye, Penelope Elmsly."

"Is that a threat?" she questioned, beginning to enjoy their game.

"It's a promise," he growled.

"Dinner is served!" Conner announced, grabbing Charlotte and Flora around their middles and dragging them toward the dining room.

"Miss Elmsly." Drummond held out his arm.

The dining room was set with a smaller table than before, making for an intimate atmosphere. Dozens of candle set the scene with a table of lush yellow roses. Penelope recalled Theodore Harrison explaining that the cheerful flowers were the symbol of friendship. As Drummond helped her to her seat and sat beside her, she pushed the thought of the English gentleman from her mind.

"Quite a fanciful spread," Penelope said, admiring the close quarters.

"Since we're leaving, there wasn't a point in leaving the large table out," Charlotte explained, motioning for the footmen to bring in the first course of pheasant soup.

Penelope stiffened. "You aren't *all* leaving, are

you?"

"Of course not," Flora said happily. "I wanted to stay on in London and dear Drum is trapped with me as my chaperone."

Penelope let out a sigh and allowed her shoulders to relax. She hadn't thought about whom else would be returning to Scotland with Conner and Charlotte. The news that Drummond would remain behind heartened her, although she'd never admit it aloud.

As they began their meal, the revelers let the drink flow, and by the third course of roast mutton, most of them were all comfortably drunk, aside from Charlotte, who merely drank water. It was an almost hilariously far cry from her pre-marriage days of drinking to abandon. As they sat and picked at their food, Drummond placed his hand on Penelope's thigh beneath the table. Through the layers of silk, his sturdy heat was still heavier than any other weight she had ever felt. He kept his fingers still and never glanced her way as he spoke to Conner. She was grateful that, with the full tablecloth, no one would have any idea of how close they were.

Before the dessert was served, Conner stood, a bit awkwardly due to drink, and clanked his spoon against his glass. "Attention family, friends, footmen. Charlotte and I have an announcement."

Charlotte smiled and finished the statement hurriedly, her mouth splitting into a wide grin. "I am with child!"

Penelope leapt from her seat and embraced her friend while Drummond and Flora applauded. "Oh, Charlotte, I'm so happy for you! Your own little

Scottish baby lord!"

"Or lady." Charlotte laughed.

Penelope inspected her torso. "I had no idea. I couldn't tell by looking at you."

"It's so new. I've been ill and fatigued. In fact, I would retire now, if I could."

"Please, go rest if you're tired! Shall I help you to the drawing room to put your feet up? Or perhaps you'd like to go straight to bed?"

"To bed, I think." Charlotte yawned. "I'm so sorry to leave you all."

"Never fear, wife," Conner said, draining the last of his whiskey and rising from his seat. "I'll take ye up. I might fall over drunk soon enough, so I might as well fall into bed."

Flora's clever blue eyes shifted around the room at each of them. "I'm rather tired, as well. Pity to miss dessert, but my bed beckons."

"Are we all goin' to bed, then?" Drummond asked in an air of affected innocence that Penelope saw through as soon as he added a wide yawn at the end.

"We're all goin' to *someone's* bed!" Conner jested, throwing his arm about his wife and leading her from the room. Flora trailed behind, humming a jaunty wedding march as she went.

"Are ye goin' to retire, as well?" Drummond asked Penelope, toying with the rim of his glass.

"I suppose I should, if everyone else is. Although, I do wish we could have celebrated the coming baby a bit more before turning in. It all seemed rather rushed."

"I'm sure ye'll have a bit o' time before they

leave tomorrow."

"So, that's it, then? They're really leaving?"

"Aye," he said, standing. "They must, especially with the babe comin'. It must be born in MacLeod lands."

"I suppose I understand."

"Come, I'll show ye to your chambers." He held out his hand this time, instead of his arm.

Fingers interlocked, they left the dining room and strolled the empty hall through the townhouse. Penelope kept her eyes open for maids and footmen, but their walk upstairs to the bedrooms was thankfully undisturbed. Although Charlotte had made it clear that things were different between men and women in Scotland, Penelope didn't fancy the thought of a maid gossiping about her in the marketplace. Everything said at the shops was always instant news.

The room she was taken to was tastefully furnished in the MacLeod blue and Penelope longed to get out of her corset, for more than one reason.

Once they were safely tucked away in Penelope's temporary quarters, Drummond pulled her to him, folding her tightly into his arms. "I've waited all night for this. Do ye have any idea how hard it is to sit beside you, barely touchin'?"

"You had your hand on my thigh all evening."

"Like I said, barely touchin'."

"I noticed that the help seems quite sparse tonight. Would you be so kind as to play lady's maid?"

"My lady." He grinned and began plucking her pins from her hair, dropping them to the floor. His fingers were quick and gentle, and as soon as her flaxen hair was loose about her face, he began deftly releasing the hooks at the back of her gown. When the dress was left to fall around her feet, he placed a light kiss upon her shoulder. Her corset swiftly followed.

Penelope debated what she was about to do. On one hand, these new feelings were deliciously wicked, and unlike any other pleasure she had ever felt before. His mere touch was enough to set her body on fire, and that was something Penelope didn't know she needed until that first night in her room. But, on the other hand, she was a highborn lady who should be safe in her own chambers, being tended to by a young ladies maid and thinking over her appropriate suitors. However, Penelope's thinking was hardly appropriate, as of late.

Drummond picked Penelope up as if she weighed nothing, and she instinctively wrapped her legs around his solid middle, her arms at his neck. He dropped her on the goose down bed, making her laugh. He stood at the edge of the bed and lifted one of her legs, hooking a finger around her French heel and tossing it to the floor. When the other one was also gone, he moved to the stockings. Slowly, he unrolled each silk hose, his hands lavishing attention on her newly bared legs.

"I could die here, now, seein' ye like this, and be a happy man."

"Well, I do hope you don't plan on dropping dead in my bedchamber. That would be rather difficult to explain to the staff."

"I would no' want to inconvenience ye." He

laughed, climbing onto the bed and hovering over her. "But I would like to make ye feel like ye would die."

"Is that so?"

"Aye," he said, running a finger down her neck and stopping at the collar of her chemise. "The French call it *la petite mort*."

"You speak French?"

He shrugged, his hands running up her thighs and to her shapely hips. "Ye pick up a few things in France. I'm no' an expert, but I know enough." Drummond pushed up the hem of her chemise. "This could never get old."

Penelope shivered in excitement, attempting to push away the dull nag of shame that pelted her mind. Instead, she tried pulling Drummond to her, hoping to lose herself in his embrace as she did the night before, but it was like trying to move a mountain. The Scot was planted between her knees, peering at her over the twin slopes of her breasts.

"No' so fast. There's work to be done here."

Her breath caught in her throat as he dipped below the edge of her shift, planting a line of kisses up her inner thighs. When his mouth found the junction of her legs, Penelope cried out in surprise, finding the new sensation of his hot mouth upon her entirely too much to bear.

"Oh, Drummond! Please!" The pleasure grew deep in her core as her fingers tangled in his thick hair. Her breath hitched in her chest as she fought for air. "Please, I need, I want—"

As she climaxed, her body craved something to fill the emptiness that grew within her. Penelope tried to tug Drummond upward by yanking upon his shirt. She succeeded in pulling the offending garment off, but still the Scot stayed between her knees, looking at her hungrily.

"If I could, I would in an instant."

"Then do it," Penelope begged, not entirely understanding what 'it' was, besides the fact that it was a sin. "Please, Drummond."

"Penelope, what do ye want to happen?" he asked, suddenly serious. "What are we doin' here?"

Her eyes widened, her mind still cloudy with the aftereffects of his oral ministrations. "What do you mean?"

"What's a proper lady doin' in bed with a title-less Scot?" Drummond leaned back on his heals, regarding her intently. He rubbed at his chin and took a deep breath in through his nose. "What is this?"

"Well…I…I mean, we're just…" She groped for the words that didn't exist. She knew that gallivanting in bed with Drummond was improper, but she found that her morals melted away the moment he settled his green gaze upon her. There were no words, no phrase, for the odd pull he had upon her and Penelope couldn't explain where things were going, nor what to call their odd relationship…if relationship wasn't too strong a word.

"Ye want me to take your maidenhead? Ruin ye for your husband?"

Penelope flushed at his harsh questioning, but there was a grave look on his face that showed his sincere concern. "Honestly, I haven't any thoughts past tonight, right now. If I think too much…I just try to stay in the moment, I suppose."

"I can no' let ye do that to yourself." Drummond pulled her shift back over her knees and stood from the bed. "I care about ye far too much to let ye give yourself to me. Ye might be new to the workin's o' the flesh, but where this would end is no' any good for ye."

She folded her legs toward her, lost for words. "I don't understand."

"I know." He ran a hand through his hair, but the russet locks fell back in his eyes. "And that's the problem. Penelope, we've let this go too far. Where we should have ended it at a bit o' harmless flirtin', we allowed to turn into somethin' that could have ended badly had it continued."

Penelope felt tears of frustration pool in her eyes and she angrily brushed them away before they could fall. "Drummond, what are you saying?"

"We can no' do this. I got carried away in my feelin's for ye." He came to stand beside her and leaned to cup her face in his hand. "I tried to ignore the reality o' what's goin' on. But, the truth o' it is that I'm nothin', I'm no one. I do no' have a castle, or money, or businesses all over London. I carry a sword and pluck a bow for my chieftain. I have nothin' but a bit o' land. I have nothin' to offer ye."

The tears flowed freely now as she clasped his hand in hers and squeezed his fingers tightly. "You're *not* nothing. You're *someone*. You're Drummond MacGregor and you have *so* much to offer. You're handsome and strong and care so deeply."

"I wish your words were true," he said quietly, dipping to kiss her upon the cheek. "But, I think it's time we both make the decision to end this. I'll make plans to leave for Scotland as soon as I'm able."

She swallowed the lump building in her throat, attempting to keep her emotions at bay. "You don't need to do that."

"Aye, but I do. I can no' keep seein' ye like this, knowin' that we come from two different worlds. It's gettin' harder for me to stay away, no' that I've been tryin' as I should."

"I don't want you to stay away."

"But I must. I need to leave London and put distance between us before either of us…I should go to my room."

Penelope found herself being hit by the reality that she would soon be alone and hot tears streamed down her face. "Please, just stay tonight."

"Penelope, I—"

"Just stay." Her voice was firmer than she felt as he slid into bed beside her and pulled her to him. She lay with her head upon his chest, committing his heartbeat to memory, and pretending that it wasn't the last time she would hear it.

Chapter Fourteen

When the carriage let Penelope out in front of her home, she couldn't wait to get up to her room and have a good cry. When she awoke that morning, Drummond had already gone, and by the time she was dressed, Conner and Charlotte were just finishing finalizing their traveling plans. The goodbyes to her best friend were painful, and when Drummond had merely nodded in her direction, averting his steely gaze, Penelope almost asked a footman to carry her to her carriage in fear she might faint.

When she entered the townhouse, her mother was all a tizzy. She began fluffing out Penelope's skirts and tucking loose hairs back under her bun.

"Mother, what are you doing?" Penelope asked wearily.

"Your future husband is in the library waiting for you!"

"You mean Theodore Harrison?"

Cecily rolled her eyes. "Whom else could I possibly be speaking of?"

"Must I entertain him now? I'm very tired."

"You most certainly will. He is the most eligible bachelor of the season and he is currently in our sitting room." She balled her fists to her hips and frowned. "I wish you had time to adequately dress, though."

"What's wrong with my dress?"

"It's just that a lighter color than that dark green would suit you so much better. You really belong in pastels. Oh, and your pearl necklace! Yes, that would have—"

"Mother, I'm already dressed and finished. Now, please let me be. There's nothing to do about it."

Cecily sniffed. "Oh, well then. I suppose you know best."

Penelope watched as her mother sauntered away toward the staircase, muttering about ungrateful daughters and respect of elders. Brushing the thoughts of her mother, and the strong, Scottish suitor away, she marched toward the sitting room, trying to force her face into a mask of pleasant beauty. If Drummond would be leaving for good, then she'd have to try to move on. Sweet Theodore Harrison, ever the gentleman, would do just as well as anyone.

"Miss Elmsly." Theodore perked up upon seeing her, a bouquet of vibrant yellow blooms tied with a white ribbon in his hand.

"Mister Harrison." Penelope allowed her hand to be kissed. "I'm so sorry if I kept you waiting. If I had known you would come to call, I would have ensured to be at home."

"Don't think of it. Your mother is the perfect

hostess," he said, handing her the fragrant blossoms. "The gorse flower represents my enduring affection for you."

Penelope smelled the tiny yellow petals. "Thank you, I've never seen such thing."

"They're just as rare and delicate as you."

"Ooh," Cecily cooed, suddenly coming into the room. Penelope wondered how the elderly matron had managed to get back in time to watch. The picture of her scrambling down the hall was borderline comical. "How delightful."

Penelope had to admit that he was a charming man. She passed the bouquet to a maid. "Please put these in some water and place them in my bedchambers."

"Miss Elmsly, would you do me the honor of allowing me to take you to tea?" Theodore asked eagerly. "I have a standing table at the Stoneward."

"That would be lovely. And I do believe my carriage is still outside."

He turned toward her mother. "Would it be acceptable to take Penelope to tea?"

"Oh, certainly, please do!" Cecily replied, her voice getting higher with each word.

She almost pushed the pair from the house in her excitement to have Penelope seen in public with Theodore. While her mother's pushiness would have usually annoyed Penelope to no end, she found that she and Theodore did get along seamlessly, with Theodore saying all the right things at all the right times. He told her of his green house plans and asked how she fancied the country. She mentioned her love of music and he offered her use of his new upright piano. By the time the carriage stopped in front of the Stoneward, Penelope found Theodore not only polite and agreeable, but also positively darling.

When a maitre'd showed them to Theodore's table, Greta Hallstone cut them off, her simpering smile not reaching her eyes.

"Penelope, dear, how lovely to see you," Greta said, her snake-like gaze upon Theodore. "I had no idea you were acquainted with Mister Harrison."

Theodore nodded to her. "Good day, Miss Hallstone. Penelope was merely kind enough to allow me the pleasure of taking tea with her."

"Oh, how…quaint." Greta sighed. "Must be nice to be treated so, after running about with all those Scots all season."

Penelope blushed in embarrassment, almost forgetting that there was no way Greta knew of her secret nights with Drummond.

"Ah, yes, the MacLeods. *Wonderful* people," Theodore said, picking an invisible puff of lint from his jacket. "I do find Scotland to be most enjoyable. Such culture and beauty in their country. Pity you don't feel the same, Miss Hallstone. But then again, only the most cultivated of us are able to truly appreciate Scotland."

"Well…I…I…" Greta's mouth flapped in that fish-like way of hers, making Penelope cover a giggle with a small cough.

"Thank you," Penelope whispered as Theodore helped her into her seat.

"Please, don't think of it. Miss Hallstone isn't a true friend to many people and for good reason. So, don't fret over her."

Penelope felt at ease now, at his words. They echoed her own about nasty Greta Hallstone the last time she came to tea. It warmed her heart, still badly bruised by Drummond's rejection. She hated how her mind kept wandering to him, especially when the man who longed to be with her was sitting right there within reach.

"Miss Elmsly," Theodore began, his hands wrapped around his teacup. "I pray I'm not being too forward, but I do hope that you enjoy spending time with me as much as I do you?"

Penelope almost laughed aloud at his idea of being forward. "Mister Harrison, I treasure our time together. You're always the perfect gentleman."

Her words seemed to please him and he sipped his tea jovially, a grin on his classically handsome face. "Then I hope you will find it agreeable for me to call upon you more often?"

"I would like that, very much."

***

Penelope sat up that night, clutching the MacGregor crest in her hand until the pointed silver cut into her skin. She had lit a candle at the window, hoping that Drummond would see it and decide to scale the walls to meet with her. They had parted on sour, wretched terms with Drummond saying they should never meet again. Still, she longed to see his familiar shape striding through the darkened roads.

As the hour grew late, she was about to blow out the candle when she saw him standing at the edge of the road, looking up toward her window. She wondered how long he had been there, watching the candle die away in the night. Penelope felt faint and backed away from the window, rushing to the mirror and checking her reflection. Her face was pink and puffed from crying that evening so she dimmed her oil lamps, hoping the subdued light would hide her grief.

"I didn't think you would come," she said quietly as Drummond shut her bedroom window behind him.

"I almost did no'," he admitted. "I must have turned back a dozen times on my way."

"I'm glad you're here. I was scared I would never see you again." Penelope wanted to go to him, but the warmth that usually radiated from his body was gone, replaced by an icy shield that chilled the air before them.

Luckily, he breached the space between them, enveloping her in a tight embrace. She melted into his arms, gripping his shoulders as she felt her body weaken. She breathed in his familiar scent, trying to commit the smell to memory. The fear that this would be their last meeting tore her soul anew.

"I know I said I would never come to ye again, but I needed to, one last time," he said into her hair.

"This doesn't need to be the end."

"Ye know it does. Ye know we can no' go on like this, sneaking about in the night when ye find a suitable husband."

"Never," she cried, burrowing her face deeper into his chest. "I can't. I'll only think of you." And, it was true. Thoughts of Drummond filled her mind most when she tried to ignore them. When at tea with Theodore, she found herself playacting, putting on a show as if she was a proper lady when all she longed to do was be abed with a Scottish warrior.

"Ye will, and ye must. I did no' come here to continue this, but to give it more closure."

"But I don't *want* closure." She looked up at him, hoping she could sway him. "I want *you.*"

Drummond's face contorted and he sat her down upon the edge of her bed. But, this time it was solemn. Gone were the playful grabs and sensual murmurs in the dark, replaced with grave seriousness of final goodbyes.

"I wanted to give ye somethin'."

"You don't need to do that," Penelope said, watching as he dug in his sporran and pulled out something small.

"I do," he replied firmly, kneeling down and taking her right hand. He pressed something onto her third finger. "There is no' much left from my clan, but I wanted to give ye this ring. It's old, but means a great deal to me."

Penelope looked down at the ring. It was a delicate thing of gold with three amethysts set in a row, offset by diamonds. "It's beautiful, but I can't accept this."

"Ye must. Please. It's all I have to give ye."

"No, it's not." Her voice cracked. "Give me you, that's all I want."

A pained look tore his features and he shook his head. "I can no'. Ye know that, even if ye can no' admit it to yourself. Please, do no' ask it o' me again. I will no' have the strength to deny ye."

Penelope nodded, trying to compose herself. She couldn't bear it if her blubbering face was the last he saw of her. She got up from the bed and went to her desk, her gaze upon the amethyst ring as she walked. She unlocked the secret compartment and withdrew the heavy stack of papers. Hands shaking, she held the notes up to him, each word carefully written and ready for the presses.

"Please, go on with this book," she pleaded. "I've drafted some letters for you to send to the publishers."

"I do no' think I could."

"Dummond, you must," she said, coming to him, forcing the papers into his hands. "We've both worked so hard. I can't see your talent go to waste."

He shook his head, looking at the floor. "I can't. It'll pain me too much."

For such a giant warrior, Penelope now saw him as something fragile. "Please, do it for me. I'll-I'll keep your ring as long as you swear to me you'll go forward with this book and see it in print."

"Will ye truly keep it?" His voice was hopeful as he turned to her, his usually vibrant eyes dull.

"Always. I only wish I had something to give you in return to remember me by."

Drummond stood, the manuscript tucked under his arm. He took her right hand and kissed the ring. "I need no token to remember ye by. I'll hear your voice in the wind that beats the thistles on the hills and think o' ye when I pass a cluster of bluebells by the loch. I'll remember your face, your skin, your taste, until my dyin' day."

Penelope's face crumpled and she clung to

Drummond as tears ran down her cheeks. She had tried, fiercely, to keep her emotions at bay, but the beauty of his words felt like a stab. He rubbed her back, murmuring soothing Scottish Gaelic words into her ear.

She found herself beginning to laugh, the painful noise creaking from her chest. "I have no idea what you're saying, but I could listen to it forever."

He dried her tears with the pad of his thumb, and tucked it under her chin to force her face upward. "I'll miss ye, Penelope Elmsly."

"And I'll miss you, Drummond MacGregor." Her whispered voice cracked.

Drummond dipped down and kissed her lightly, softly, pouring the unsaid emotions through his lips. Penelope held in fresh sobs at the finality of the gesture. Neither had any more words to offer the other. Instead, they settled on standing in silence, regarding each other with a deep sorrow neither would adequately portray.

Silently, he released her and crossed to the window, leaping over the ledge to make his final descent. Penelope darted toward the sill, leaning over to watch his departure. She wanted to see him for as long as she could. Then, her hand hit something on the sill and knocked it to the floor. It was the MacGregor pin. In the miserable excitement and sorrow of the midnight meeting, Penelope hadn't remembered to return his crest.

"Drummond!" she called out, no longer caring who heard her.

He turned up to her in the shadows of the lamplight of the lane below.

"Your pin!"

"Keep it," he replied. Then the gentle Scotsman spun on his heel, melting into the darkness from which he came.

Penelope's mouth opened involuntarily, releasing a wretched howl that came from deep in her core. Drummond MacGregor was gone for good.

Chapter Fifteen

Penelope stayed in bed the following day, crying one moment and fighting the urge to follow Drummond to Scotland the next. She sent the morning maid away, feigning illness, and asked not to be disturbed. The mere thought of food turned her stomach. She lay curled beneath the covers, clutching the pin and staring at the amethyst ring upon her hand.

She wasn't sure how to feel. Charlotte going to Scotland was something Penelope was sure would upset her, and it did, but the loss of Drummond felt like a gaping wound, festering, burning. It was almost surreal to think she would never see him again or, worse, meet him one day when the MacLeods returned from Scotland. Penelope couldn't imagine sitting next to him at the dining table, pretending there was never anything between them.

As the day crept toward nightfall, her mother knocked upon the door. "Darling, may I come in?"

Penelope slipped the crest beneath her pillow and

dried her cheeks. "Enter!"

Cecily frowned as she came in to the cave-like room. She twitched open the heavy curtains to let in some light and regarded Penelope with concern. "Feeling any better?"

"I'm all right, just a bit under the weather."

Her mother smiled and held out a bouquet of small purple flowers in a miniature vase.

"Let me guess," Penelope said wearily, "Theodore Harrison?"

"Yes. He stopped by to call but I had to send him away," she said, offering her a hastily written card. "I told him you were indisposed in bed and he implored me for a pen to write to you. Very romantic."

Penelope unfolded the card, the purple blooms in one hand.

Miss Elmsly,

It pains me to hear you are unwell this day. I shall pray for a hasty recovery as much for your health, as for my own selfish need to gaze upon you. The pansies I bring says all that is needed. You occupy my waking thoughts.

Your devoted, faithful, and eager servant,

Theodore Harrison

"Isn't it lovely?" Cecily sighed.

Penelope pinked, folding up the paper. "Mother,

you can't go about reading my mail!"

"It's not as if it were sealed."

She rolled her eyes, placing the flowers on her nightstand. "Well, in the future, I would appreciate you letting me read my own letters first."

"Well, pardon me for taking an interest in my only daughter's life."

Penelope groaned, lying back amongst the pillows. "I'll send him a card later."

"Will you accept him to come to call tomorrow? He was quite insistent that he hear from you."

"I suppose," she mumbled, dragging herself from her bed and going to the desk. "I'll pen him a note and send it off with a maid."

Sated, Cecily left the room, presumably to go find Edmund's mail to read. Penelope waited until the door was closed to open up her desk and pull out her floral stationary. She found the little pink roses upon the paper slightly ironic, and vaguely wondered what Theodore Harrison would think about her choice of flowers.

Pushing the hair from her red-rimmed eyes, she began to write.

Mister Harrison,

I am sorry to have missed your visit, but thank you so much for the flowers. They are beautiful, as always. I will be in better health tomorrow and look forward to your call.

Yours,

Penelope Elmsly

She folded the note, not bothering to seal it, before calling for a maid. Once the letter was gone, and on its way to the Harrison townhouse, Penelope allowed herself to wallow. She knew that it was silly to be so torn about Drummond's return to Scotland. Even while she pleaded for him to stay, she understood that he was right when he said he had nothing to offer her. Midnight meetings were not enough to build a life on, even with her handsome dowry.

Penelope spun the ring on her ringer, trying to turn her despair into anger. It would be easier to forget Drummond if her heart was broken from rage instead of crippling grief. She focused on how quickly he left her at their final meeting, instead of at least prolonging their goodbye. But even when trying to force the fury to build within her, she still heard his mournful singing in her ears, calling her to Scotland.

***

Penelope took a deep breath, straightening her hat in the mirror. She had done a lot of reflecting the previous night and couldn't bear to think about Drummond a moment longer. As much as it pained her to admit it, he was gone and Theodore Harrison was there for her. He was always a gentleman, and if Drummond was too stupid to know what a beautiful, rich, intelligent woman had to offer, then blast him!

"Darling, are you all right?" Cecily asked. "Your cheeks are red and your nostrils are flared like a common filly's."

She turned from the mirror. "I'm fine, Mother."

"Are you nervous about Mister Harrison coming to call?"

"Yes, I suppose so," Penelope lied, hearing two sets of footsteps coming down the hall.

"Mister Theodore Harrison," the butler announced as he opened the drawing room doors.

Theodore entered with flowers tucked under one arm. "Miss Elmsly, I'm so pleased that you are well."

"Thank you, Mister Harrison." Penelope forced herself to smile and hoped the gesture didn't come out as mechanical as it felt.

He held out the vibrant pink blooms. "I just cut these from the greenhouse. Magenta zinnias represent lasting affection." His brown eyes crinkled at the edges when he smiled, warming Penelope a little.

"You are always so terribly thoughtful," she said, touching one of the petals with the tip of a finger. And he was. He always handpicked a special symbol pertaining to her for every meeting. Bless him, the man tried. A maid took the flowers away to her bedchambers to join the rest. "I did mean to ask, what do pink roses represent? I thought of you when I used my stationary, but realized that I never gave any thought to the meaning."

Theodore grinned at being invited to speak on his favorite subject. "I thought the pink roses were a grand choice for you, as they symbolize grace and sweetness."

"That's my Penelope!" Cecily chimed in shrilly.

Penelope had almost forgotten her mother was lurking in the shadows, her trusty fan at hand for any sudden swoons.

"Rightly so, Madam," he said, nodding toward her. "Miss Elmsly, I know it's terribly short notice, but I have two box seats for an early theatrical performance this afternoon. If we leave soon, we could make it to the theater with time to spare."

"That would be delightful, Mister Harrison."

"My carriage is just outside," he said, holding out his arm. When Penelope took it, Theodore glanced down at her hand. "Striking ring, Miss Elmsly. Family heirloom?"

Penelope bit her lip. "Yes. Yes, it is."

"It suits you well."

The ride to the theater was pleasant, as was the show, and the carriage ride back. Penelope strained to keep her mind upon her beau, but thoughts of Drummond kept slipping in through the cracks. Both men were so different, but each had their own advantages. While she firmly declined to think too much into Drummond's finer attributes, she focused instead on Theodore's.

"A penny for your thoughts?" he asked as he helped her from the carriage in front of Carrington's Hotel for dinner.

"Oh, I was thinking about how lovely the play was. I do adore the classics."

"Yes, *Richard III* is one of Shakespeare's finer works. I do love that you can appreciate real theater. Some ladies can speak of nothing more than parties and frocks."

"I do enjoy those, as well." Penelope giggled,

almost feeling guilty for allowing herself some fun.

"Miss Elmsly," Theodore began as they sat across from each other, "if you would allow me some more freedom to be forward, I would like to know more about your hopes for the future."

"My hopes for the future?"

"I know it's improper of me to ask, but I long to hear what it is you want in life."

Penelope paused. She recalled speaking to Charlotte about what she once wanted—a handsome and rich husband who adored her, a home in the city and country, a flock of beautiful children. But she was no longer sure if she needed all of those requirements in order to be happy. "Well, Mister Harrison, that is a difficult question to answer. I'd like to travel, get married, and have a family—generally be content with my lot in life, surrounded by the people I love."

He nodded thoughtfully. "Those are modest but admirable desires. I, too, hope to start a family with someone one day."

At his words, Penelope pinked, knowing he meant her.

Chapter Sixteen

Penelope sat before the picture window in her family's small library when her mother came in, the corners of her lips curled and her cheeks deeply flushed.

"Darling, did you know that Mister Harrison's birthday is coming up soon?"

"Is it?" she asked, not looking up from her novel. As much as she was sure Theodore Harrison would have a delightful party when the time came, she found it difficult to muster the energy to feel particularly elated for him.

"Yes. Wouldn't you like to go get him a little something?"

"Wouldn't that be improper?"

"Hardly! It's not as if you're strangers. Why don't you go on to the arcade and pick him out a little something?"

"Now?"

"Of course, *now*. Your father just received several shipments of goods, so hurry, and you'll get the first pick!" Her mother plucked the book from

Penelope's hand. "Now, run along and get dressed. Your blue Russian frock perhaps? Very fetching."

Penelope groaned and trudged up to her room, beckoning for her lady's maid. When her hair was sufficiently tucked beneath a hat and she was dressed in a cream dress—not blue, merely to spite her mother—she called for a carriage and went to the arcade.

The store was surprisingly empty. Usually, in the middle of the day, shoppers would be bustling about the main floor, fighting politely over the last silk ribbons or maxing out their credit by buying the newest dinner gloves. There were a few wayward purchasers, but Penelope still thought the sparseness odd.

To the task at hand, she wasn't sure what to do. While she had gone to the theater and had tea with Theodore Harrison, she didn't really know too much about him. They spoke of gardens, the weather, and many other respectable topics. Penelope couldn't truly say what he liked nor disliked outside of a few generic things. It was rather frustrating, to say the least.

Feeling discouraged, she tried to focus again on his good attributes, hoping to draw inspiration from her thoughts. He was a fine dancer and cut a trim figure in a morning coat. He also had very kind eyes, and treated Penelope like a queen. Surely he was a stable man who could support her in the manner she desired. She even felt confident that, if they were to continue to become intimately acquainted, he wouldn't abandon her.

Penelope plucked an ornamental cigar case from

a display but quickly returned it, as she had never known Theodore to smoke as some other men did. As she passed a stack of new umbrellas she began to feel a bit more positive about Theodore Harrison. He was a steady man, an honest man—a man she wouldn't need to coax to stay, nor beg to love her. Penelope thought that her British beau might be able to give her everything she needed, and more.

An array of leather bound books caught her eye. Each had a gold embossed flower on the cover. When Penelope flipped one open, it had the historical significance of each bloom. The next she sampled was an encyclopedia on their meanings. As she signed her name on the shop ledger while the volumes were packed in paper, Penelope felt her lips curl into the first true smile in days.

***

As she exited the Elmsly carriage, Penelope was surprised to see Theodore's own parked beside the gardens that led up to the front door. She went up the stairs, followed by a footman carrying her purchases. Her parents stood in the entryway with him, all three turning at once when she entered as if she was unexpected in her own home.

"Miss Elmsly, I'm so pleased that I caught you." Theodore smiled, the emotion reaching his eyes in such a way that he reminded her of a hopeful puppy begging to be loved.

She allowed him to kiss her gloved hand. "Mister Harrison, it is I who am pleased. I was out selecting a gift for your birthday. May I bestow it upon you presently?"

His grin widened. "My dear Miss Elmsly, you honor me."

"I do hope you like them." She motioned for the footman to come forward and unwrap the books one by one. Penelope passed each, in turn, to Theodore for his inspection. "When I saw them, I knew at once that they were for you."

"Wherever did you find such wondrous volumes?" His child-like eagerness charmed her. He appreciated her efforts, even the small ones.

"At my father's arcade." She was about to ask her father if there were any more, but noted that her parents were gone. "Oh, I hadn't noticed my parents left. But I'll be sure to ask my father if there are any more in the collection."

Theodore passed the books back to the footmen with an order to have them placed in his carriage. "Miss Elmsly, would you care to come with me to see a new greenhouse that I've been participating in?"

"Certainly. I'll just check in with my parents."

"No need. They're the ones who suggested that I take you out," he told her, still in a jovial mood that Penelope found rather infectious.

As they rode toward the greenhouse, she watched as Theodore flipped through one of the books, his eyes lighting up when he came upon a particularly titillating plant. His enthusiasm was uplifting and she felt a peculiar sense of pride when he declared her gift the best he had ever received. But still, she felt guilty with the Scottish ring wrapped around her finger and hidden by a glove.

"This is just a small show of what I plan to do," Theodore told her as he led her to a nondescript brick building. The inside looked like some sort of library, but once they reached the back, she could barely contain her awe.

The domed ceiling of the greenhouse was entirely glass, as were the walls, and the scent of fresh blooms permeated the air, crisp and mouthwateringly sweet. The leaves were a luscious green that almost seemed to reflect light and Penelope spied plants she had never seen before. The foliage was so thick, she wondered if it were possible to fully explore.

"Goodness," she muttered, peering closely at a bright pink flower with pointed petals. "It's all so marvelous."

"Do you really like it?"

"It's amazing." The carefully manicured gardens of the country were different than this stunningly wild display. "It's like a miniature jungle here."

"I set out with much different ideas of how I would cultivate this greenhouse, but found myself inspired." He steered her around the edge of the conservatory walls. "The untamed beauty of these plants remind me so much of you."

Penelope blushed, looking away from his earnest expression. "Oh, you do flatter me."

"No, I tell you the truth." He brought her to a stop at the back of the greenhouse. "This is all for you."

Lined up against a glass wall sat dozens of flowers, carefully potted and pruned. She recognized several from his many offerings to her, and her mother. Penelope was deeply touched to know that the blooms had come from his own hard work, and not from one of London's many florists.

"There are all the blossoms I've already given you, and above us are the flowers I'd like to gift you next.

Penelope glanced upward to see they stood under several blooming orange trees, the orange blossoms flourishing to bright bursts of white. She smiled and breathed in deeply.

"Mister Harrison, this is all so beautiful. Thank you." Penelope sighed, touching the petals of a low hanging fruit.

"This is how it could always be." He drew closer. "Our world could be touched by orange blossoms and exotic foliage. Our lives could be beautiful, and together we could make a brilliant garden of our own. That is, if you'll have me?"

Her mouth dropped open in a way she was sure wasn't becoming. "Have you?"

Theodore drew down to one knee and pulled a box from his coat pocket, holding it out to her with steady hands. "Miss Elmsly…*Penelope*…you are the finest, most darling, cheerful soul I've ever met. Every moment with you has been positive perfection and I couldn't imagine experiencing life without you by my side. Will you marry me?"

Penelope thought she might faint. Her stomach churned and she struggled to bring his face back into focus. "*Marry* you? Do you mean it?"

"A man doesn't dip to his knees in a new suit merely for a jest." He shot out a hand for her to hold and his sturdy grip stabilized her.

"Oh, Mister Harrison, this is all so sudden," she cried out, both excited and frightened beyond belief. She knew he was enamored with her, but had no idea that thoughts of marriage were already on his mind. She should have been thrilled about being proposed to in such a wonderful way, but she couldn't clear her mind and focus on the present.

"It isn't sudden for me. I've known it was you, and only you, since we first met. The moment I saw you in that ballroom and we shared our first dance, I became intoxicated by your grace and felt the desire to take you as my wife. That is why I pursued you so valiantly. I needed to make you mine before any other man had the chance."

"Mister Harrison…I…" She felt her mouth go dry and her corset suddenly seemed too tight as the air continued to be sucked from her lungs.

"Penelope, you torture me." He looked up at her, his eyes pleading. "Please, Penelope, be my wife? I cannot bear this life without you."

Her mind spun and images rushed through her head—meeting Drummond, starting their book together, their midnight meetings, and the fateful night he banished himself from her life. She felt a pain in her chest as these visions arose. She tucked them back, cursing the Scot and praising the fine, British gentleman who loved her enough to take her to wife. Finally, it would be her turn to be the blushing bride with a handsome husband to quiet all those who gossiped about her.

"Oh, Theodore, I will!" she exclaimed enthusiastically, feeling her breath rush back into her chest.

Grinning a toothy smile, he rose from his knee, opening the box in his hand. "I hope that you like it." He opened the box showing a sizable amethyst.

Penelope felt a lump in her throat upon seeing the purple stone set in a silver filigree band. It was decadent, flashy, and fine enough to make anyone jealous. But seeing it pained her. "An amethyst?"

"Yes! You looked so fine with the other ring you wear that, when I saw this, I just *knew* you were made to be an amethyst bride." He looked so proud as he slipped the ring over her gloved hand it nearly broke her heart anew. "Just as I thought it would be—a perfect fit. Just like us."

***

Theodore, as he implored her to address him, chattered through the whole ride back to the Elmsly townhome. He spoke of how proud his mother would be—she was in Germany visiting relatives—and the kind of life they would have. Seasons in town and a country home to entertain in between jaunts to Bali and Bombay. Theodore made their future lives seem lively and full of family, friends, and several children who would receive all the looks, breeding, and money their parents had to offer.

He spoke with such honest excitement that Penelope found it hard to think of anything else. As much as she grieved the loss of Drummond, he was gone and left her fully broken. There was no chance for him to return to her, a lone figure standing beneath the lamppost, looking up at her bedroom window. Theodore, a darling man, saw her for the treasure she was and had so many spectacular plans for their future. She smiled at him from her seat, both hands heavy with amethysts from two very different men.

As soon as the carriage stopped before her house, Penelope could see the window dressings of the drawing room twitch. She sighed, not looking forward to the barrage that was about to befall her. Her mother was surely bubbling over with anticipation at the thought of her bagging such a fine husband. She almost wished she could have Theodore order the carriage to circle the block, just to twist her mother's arm, but he was already helping her down to the sidewalk. They had been spotted and there was no turning back.

"Penelope!" Cecily rushed through the front door, clinging to her, fat tears rolling down her cheeks as she sobbed dramatically. "My dear daughter!"

"Mother." Penelope blushed, embarrassed with such an obnoxious show of affection in public. "Might we go inside?"

"Oh, yes. Yes!" She pulled them both into the house where a butler stood, holding a tray of champagne. "Let us have a toast. Edmund? *Edmund*!"

He stepped out of an adjoining room a moment later. "Yes? Oh! Mister Harrison, Penelope, I anticipate that congratulations are in order?"

"They are." Theodore glanced fondly toward Penelope. "Your daughter has agreed to be my wife."

"Jolly good!" Edmund shook his hand firmly. "Glad to have you!"

Penelope smiled politely as the two men passed compliments and Cecily cried into her lace handkerchief, blubbering about napkins and flower arrangements. Ordinarily, Penelope would have loved to go over fabric samples and talk about guest lists, but now she was itching to write to Charlotte. Having her dearest friend so far away was painful and she wished she were back in London to help her deal with her conflicting emotions.

"I do hate to cut this happy time off, but I am expected in my London offices," Theodore said the moment there was a lull in the conversation.

Cecily gasped. "Surely not on the very eve of your engagement!"

"I am afraid so."

"Don't give Harrison a hard time," Edmund said, slapping his future son-in-law on the back. "He must keep business going."

"How else can I afford to take my wife on an extended honeymoon tour of Europe?" Theodore grinned at Penelope.

"Europe?" she asked, feeling a smile curl her lips.

He nodded and paused a moment, thinking. "We'll go to France to start and then to Germany in time for the fall festivals. From there we'll travel through Austria to Italy and take a steamship to Spain."

"Spain?" she whispered, her heart racing at the list of exotic destinations.

"Yes, Spain. Then we'll be back in London in

time for Christmas, and the society season, of course." He nodded toward Edmund. "I was thinking that afterward your parents might like to accompany us to the East Indies to stock up on products for the arcade. I keep a small estate in Bombay for business."

"You've certainly thought this out." Penelope felt a wave of confused emotions wash over her.

"I am nothing but a planner, my dear." He then took her hand and bowed over it, kissing it gently. "Now, I must take my leave."

Penelope was secretly thankful Theodore didn't stay long. She yearned to escape and process everything that had happened. Cecily was just beginning to stifle her tears as the butler closed the front door behind her fiancé. As soon as her mother was about to let loose a new wave of happy cries, Penelope dashed up the stairs to her room, locking herself in to avoid the wedding talk.

She needed time alone to deal with all the changes that were rapidly occurring in her life. She pulled off her engagement ring and both her gloves, seeing Drummond's Scottish jewels tight around her finger. She found it grotesquely humorous that Theodore had chosen amethyst based on the ring she already wore. Of course he would have no idea the meaning behind the stones, but Penelope felt guilty about betraying him.

She sat down at her writing desk and pulled out a piece of stationary. The pen hovered over the paper as she thought of the words to say. She longed to tell Charlotte the truth of it, the truth of everything. If anyone would understand her longing for a

Scottish man, it would be her, but she couldn't bring herself to write the words. There was nothing to be done about Drummond and Penelope certainly wouldn't be the sort of woman to pine after a man.

My dearest Charlotte,

Exciting news! I am engaged to be married to Theodore Harrison with a wedding to follow in several weeks, as soon as it can be sorted. I know that it is terribly short notice, and you only just arrived back in Scotland, but I cannot imagine being wed without you here with me. Please come back with Conner and Flora, if you are able!

All my love,

Penelope

As she folded up the letter to be taken to the mail, her Scottish ring caught the light from the window, flashing brightly, reminding her of its presence. She stroked the purple and clear stones, wishing to feel Drummond's aura surround her. As much as she didn't want to think of the handsome Scot who taught her to let go, she found it almost impossible not to feel her heartbreak every time she saw the ring on her hand. It was a constant reminder of the almost-love she had lost forever.

Biting her lip to fight back the tears, she knew it wasn't fair to Theodore to begin married life in Drummond's shadow. He was a good man who deserved a devoted wife who didn't wear his ring on one hand, and her old lover's on another. The tears tumbled down her cheek as she slipped Drummond's gift from her finger, rubbing at the faint indentation it left behind, feeling dejected as she knew it would quickly fade.

She took a tiny key, unlocked the secret compartment in her desk, and placed the Scottish gems in the small space alongside the MacGregor pin, vowing to never wear it again. Penelope couldn't bear to rid herself of it entirely, but knew it must be all but forgotten. And as she locked the compartment, hiding the ring away, she also imprisoned a piece of her heart.

Chapter Seventeen

Penelope sat in the library with her mother, samples of table linins spread on her father's desk. It had been a week since Theodore's proposal and wedding planning was swiftly moving forward. The moment he'd left, that day, Cecily had sent out to the printer for cards announcing the couple's engagement. Anyone who was anyone in London society promptly received the news as quickly as Cecily could send her footmen to deliver it.

"Pale pink or pale yellow?" Cecily held up two napkins.

"Pink."

"Gold cutlery, or silver?"

"Gold." Penelope picked at the formal invitation sample, already set with their names, a ring of painted orange blossoms trimming the fine paper.

Cecily sighed, putting down the pen in her hand. "Penelope, is something the matter?"

"No, why would you think that?"

"You've always been such a fan of party planning. Why, when Charlotte came to plan her wedding, you basically had everything selected before she even stepped foot in London."

"It's different planning for someone else's wedding. It's easier."

"What's easier than being a bride?" She threw her hands up theatrically. "All you need to do is select everything you ever wanted and have it handed to you on a silver platter! Speaking of platters, I need a list of food for the reception. I'm thinking duck."

A footman slipped into the room, a letter for Penelope on his tray. When she saw the MacLeod seal on the envelope, she eagerly tore it open.

Penelope,

We are all very happy for you to have received such a fine proposal! Theodore Harrison seems a perfect gentleman and I'm sure he'll make a wonderful husband. Conner is gone north to inspect the borderlands and I am having a difficult time with the pregnancy. Unfortunately, my physician believes I should not be traveling until after the baby is born, so it'll be impossible for me to come. I am so sorry that I can't be there, but I will leave for London as soon as I am able in order to properly celebrate with you. Please write me with all the wondrous details so

I might feel as if I'm there with you, instead of cloistered in bed. Dear Flora is beside herself with excitement for the chance to return to London and will leave for the first available train. A maid will accompany her as a chaperone this visit.

Love, love, love

Charlotte

Penelope's face fell and her stomach knotted. The fact that her dearest friend in the world would not be there on her wedding day seemed almost unholy. Of course it wasn't Charlotte's fault, and the health of the newest MacLeod took rightful precedence over her nuptials, but it still stung dreadfully. They had always done everything together, and how she felt so alone.

"Bad news?" Cecily asked, peering at her over the frames of her reading spectacles.

Penelope passed her the note and crossed her arms. "Charlotte can't attend the wedding."

Cecily scanned the letter, her frown deepening with each line. "Dear, I am ever so sorry. I know you wish she could be here." She took Penelope's hand, dislodging it from its place by her side. "Perhaps you might ask darling Theodore if he would consider stopping by Scotland during your honeymoon? It's only a short detour on your trip and I'm certain he'd be more than agreeable."

"Mother, that's a brilliant idea." She brightened

considerably. Theodore was planning a jaunt around Europe that would last a few months and, surely, he wouldn't mind a detour to visit her oldest friend. He was very agreeable in that sense. However, the thought of sitting down at a dinner table with her husband on one side, and her old lover on another, seemed too terrible to even think about. Nonetheless, her desire to see Charlotte trumped any awkwardness of seeing *him*.

"Now that that's settled, can we please speak of more dire matters?" Cecily asked, her face a mask of seriousness. "Hors d'oeuvres!"

***

"Pardon me, Miss Elmsly." A butler cleared his throat, interrupting Penelope's casual dinner alone in the dining room. "There's a young Miss MacLeod here to call. Are you at home to receive her?"

Penelope threw down her napkin and leaped up from her seat so quickly, she nearly knocked it over. "I'm always at home for any of the MacLeods!"

She rushed to the entryway to see Flora, her hair loose around her shoulders. She wore a gray traveling gown and was, as always, the perfect mix of a wild Scottish woman and a noble lady.

Penelope threw her arms around her, and she reciprocated the hug, tightly squeezing her round her slim middle. "Oh, Flora, I'm so glad you've come! Ever so happy!"

"And miss a chance to attend some of your amazing bashes? Not likely!"

"Come, eat, I was just sitting down to dine." Penelope pulled her back down the hall to the dining room, ordering a footman to pile Flora's plate high. "Tell me everything. How's Charlotte? Is she well? How's Scotland? Was your trip calm?"

"Goodness, you'd think you haven't seen another person in ages!" Flora giggled, spearing some food with her fork. "Well, Charlotte is mostly abed and very ill, but the doctors assure us it's perfectly normal for a pregnancy. Scotland is wet and green, as always, and I had a lovely trip here."

"I'm glad to hear her pregnancy is coming along, even if it sounds rather unpleasant. But I'm so pleased that she's sent you back to be with me."

"I haven't missed your engagement dinner, have I?"

"No, it's in two nights, so you're just in time."

Flora grinned, swallowing her bite. "I'm glad to hear it! I do love the English parties. As soon as Charlotte got your letter, I began to pack for a lengthy stay. I longed to return to London and you getting married was the perfect excuse to come."

"I'm merely an excuse to come rejoin society?" Penelope gasped jokingly. "Flora, I'm shocked."

She flicked a pea at her. "You know I wanted to come and see you, as well. No need to go to seed over it, you goose. Anyone with any sense in their head would miss you the moment you walked from a room."

Penelope bit the inside of her cheek, trying to keep herself from keep from asking about the one person she dared not speak of again. But Flora was much more perceptive than anyone gave her credit for.

"He's all right," she said quietly, all MacLeod mirth gone from her eyes as she pushed the remainders of her meal about her plate. "He's more quiet than before, less quick to smile, but he's well enough considering the circumstances."

"Thank you." She averted her gaze, trying to hide her tears.

"He's sent something along with me and asked me to give it to you."

Penelope looked up, almost shocked but also more excited than she would ever admit. It gave her a pang of guilt deep in her belly. "Really?"

"Yes." Flora asked a footman to deliver the item from her carriage and he promptly returned with a paper-wrapped package under his arm. "I almost didn't bring it. I didn't know if you'd want to see it."

"I do," she breathed. "I need to see it." The emotion was palpable as her fingers shook upon touching the gift. She was almost frightened to unwrap the paper, not knowing what it held. She had thought she had locked away Drummond, along with the ring. But now he was back in her home, in her hands, and she was almost too scared to go forward.

"Open it," Flora prompted, her face pale and still.

Penelope took a deep breath and peeled it all away, leaving her with a lush, pale blue, book. The edges were trimmed in gold and *Tales and Music of the MacGregor Clan* was embossed on the cover. She held back a sob as she stroked the soft leather and Flora left her seat to stand beside her, placing her hand comfortingly upon her shoulder.

"You should continue and open the book," Flora told her quietly, "if you want to."

"I don't know if I can."

"I think that you must."

"It's a beautiful color," she said, trying to stall.

Flora cleared her throat and looked around a moment before setting her gaze back on Penelope. "Drum said it was the same shade as your eyes…he helped work the leather himself to ensure it was a match."

She swallowed a sob. "That sounds like him."

"Please, open it. You really should."

Penelope knew she was right. She flipped open the cover, a smile touching her lips when she saw the name Drummond MacGregor displayed proudly in deep filigree. Seeing it written out was beautiful in the strangest way. It brought him to life in her dining room—a shadowy figure in a kilt with bright, cat-like eyes staring into her heart.

But the next page, she knew, was for her. On a sheet all its own were her initials. ***P.E.*** was centered by a cluster of painted heather with a Gaelic phrase printed beneath: ***mo anam buin ri sibh.***

"What does it mean?" Her voice cracked as she stood on the edge of devastation. "Tell me."

"*Mo anam buin ri sibh,*" Flora said, the musical Gaelic washing over Penelope like a melodic caress. "My soul belongs to you."

"My soul belongs to you." Penelope's voice cracked slightly as she struggled to contain the waves of despair that threatened to pull her under.

She gripped the book tightly, a pale lifesaver.

"I'm very sorry I had to be the one to give you that, but I promised I would deliver it." Flora shifted from foot to foot, probably uncomfortable at being the messenger of that devastating blow.

"I'm not angry with you. I'm grateful, *so* grateful. I just…I need…" She covered up a short sob with a cough and squared her shoulders, setting her chin. She had always prided herself on being poised and controlled in public but found herself slipping when confronted with whispers from Scotland. "I need to go lie down. I'm suddenly feeling rather unwell."

"Shall I come with you? Or maybe call for someone to help you to your room?" Flora asked. Penelope thought her tone was sympathetic, sad, and she couldn't handle having someone pity her.

"I'm quite all right, I just need to retire. Please excuse me."

"I'll call upon you tomorrow," Flora promised with a quick kiss on her temple.

She nodded and gave her a brief shadow of a smile before shambling from the room, fighting back hot tears as she hurried toward her chambers. No one would be allowed to watch her break, though she wasn't sure she'd be able to contain the multitudes of emotion that welled within her once she was alone.

As soon as she'd locked the door behind her, Penelope fell into bed, clutching the book to her chest, breathing in the scent of ink and freshly dyed leather. She longed to read it, to pore over the pages of texts she had lovingly compiled with Drummond, but hated the thought of breaking the spine. It was silly to worry about such a trivial thing and she almost broke out into hysterical laughter at the ridiculous thought, but the dry humor was quickly squashed by the thought of Drummond making Flora swear to deliver the volume into her hands.

Penelope could imagine him pacing, the book tucked under one large arm, wondering what to do next. She questioned if he had wanted to send a note along, or bring the book to her himself. She hadn't even had the time to ask Flora if there was a message, but doubted it. The book said everything, and more, to her very soul. Drummond had technically been good to his word that he would stay out of her life forever.

Book the book complicated manners. Did he send it to spite her? To show that he cared? How could he expect her to move on when he wrote such a devastating line to her in his book?

She silently cursed him, and his beautiful words, before falling into a new sea of tears that streamed down her face, staining her silk pillows. She missed him. God, she missed him. Every morning, in that fleeting moment between sleep and wakefulness, Penelope swore she felt his hand on her cheek and his comfortable weight beside her in bed. But when she opened her eyes, she was left with nothing more than the evanescent scent of wood smoke and Scotland he left behind.

Penelope could do little more than think as she stroked Drummond's book. She had thought she was strong enough, faithful enough, woman enough to erase him from her life to start anew on her wedding day, but she couldn't. His voice echoed in her ears, full of soft Gaelic and tender words only spoken between lovers.

She curled her body around the soft leather, then whispered, "And my soul belongs to you."

Chapter Eighteen

"Penelope, I'm very glad you agreed to meet me for tea," Flora said, taking her seat at the table.

The Stoneward was brimming with people, but Penelope had never felt so alone. "Of course. I needed to escape. I'm very sorry for running out on you yesterday, it was very rude."

"Don't think of it. But are you all right?" Flora's voice was low and her fair brows were knitted with worry.

"Might I speak candidly?" she asked delicately, her eyes scanning the room for anyone who might try to listen.

"Please."

"I'm not," she said simply, spinning her engagement ring around her finger. It fit well enough, but not as well as Drummond's had.

"I could tell. You're pale and your eyes make it look as if you didn't sleep."

"Because I didn't."

Flora frowned. "You need to take care of yourself."

"I know. I just…I'm having trouble finding a way to be all right with this. With all of this. I need to move on with my life and keep to my commitments."

"You wouldn't need to put this behind you," Flora told her, taking her hand and covering up her engagement ring with the pad of her thumb. "If you just wrote to Drummond, he'd come in a heartbeat to get you."

"I can't." It pained her to say, but she knew their parting was for the best, no matter the agony it caused her.

"You could come with us to Scotland and live in the castle. Charlotte would love having you, as would I. And you and Drum can have a grand wedding on the hills like Charlotte and Conner had with their hand fasting."

Penelope swallowed her tears. "That would be beautiful."

"Then, come. We'll go to your house and write to him straightaway," Flora said eagerly.

"No. As much as I want to, I can't just run off to Scotland."

"But why?"

"We're from two different worlds. So, please, after this meeting I need to never speak of him again. Promise me you'll hold to that?"

Flora grimaced. "I promise. Would you speak of him now, then?"

Penelope bit her lip and kept her mouth closed until the butler who served their tea and cakes left again. "I shouldn't, but if I don't, I fear the thoughts will eat me alive."

Flora pulled her hand away and wrapped it around her teacup. "I'll answer any questions you have."

She tried to sort through her feelings and push back the bitter musings of abandonment, hoping to bring more pleasant topics to mind. She couldn't risk sobbing over her teacake. Blasted Greta Hallstone would never let her forget it. "The book, it's been properly published and distributed?"

Flora nodded and poured cream into her tea before replying. "Yes. It was printed as soon as we arrived back in Scotland and is now being distributed in the main ports. Last I heard, it was doing well at home and there was talk of wider circulation."

"He must be very proud," she said quietly, her heart swelling with secondhand pride. "Will he write more? Work on more music?"

"He hasn't sung since we left London."

Penelope felt a lump in her throat. "That's terrible."

"It's not your fault. I know you asked him to stay. He told me so on the train back home." Flora reached over to a plate of cookies. "He couldn't. I think both of you are just scared."

She ignored Flora's last statement. "You two talked about me?"

"Not a lot." She averted her eyes. "Once we left the train, he asked to not have to speak about you again."

"What did you say? What did *he* say?"

"A wee bit and then some. He loved you, Penelope, even if he didn't tell you so. I know it hurts you to hear, but you wanted honesty."

"I know. What else?" Penelope was eager for information and welcomed each stinging revelation Flora brought her.

"This book won't be his last. The next, already ordered by the publishing house, is a book of sonnets—love songs. He has no one to write the music, though. None of us are practiced enough to create something new like you had. Besides, he's taking his time of it, now."

"Is he…is he all right?"

Flora shrugged, sipping at her tea. "As well as he can be, I suppose. He no longer spars with the men when he can help it. He spends a lot of time by the loch, alone, or riding in the hills. I think it helps to clear his mind."

Penelope recalled some of his parting words to her. *"I'll hear your voice in the wind that beats the thistles on the hills and think o' ye when I pass a cluster of bluebells by the loch."* She wondered if that's why he chose to seclude himself so. "Do you think he'll sing again?"

"I hope so. He has a lovely voice. It would be a shame to squander his gift."

"He does," she whispered. "I miss it so."

They sat together in silence, each sipping at the tea. Penelope forgot to add cream and sugar, but drank it nonetheless, letting the scalding liquid burn her throat. She welcomed the sharp sting, a slight punishment for the pain she caused Drummond.

Flora put down her teacup and cleared her throat. "Is that it, then?"

"That's it," Penelope affirmed.

"Then tell me of your fiancé. I want to know all about Theodore Harrison." She smiled warmly, steering the conversation back to a safe topic.

"Well, honestly, I don't suppose I know him exceedingly well. But he's generous and thoughtful, maybe to a fault."

"Always a good thing when it comes from a husband to his wife."

She nodded, digging deep, trying to focus on Theodore. "He's also passionate and—"

"Ooh, passionate!" Flora giggled.

Penelope felt heat rise into her cheeks. "Goodness, no, not like that! I mean about the things he likes."

"Like *you*?"

"No, I mean like…flowers."

"Flowers," she repeated, her face twisted into a look that was both humorous and slightly disgusted. "So, he's passionate about plants and not his fiancé?"

Penelope bit her lip, feeling slighted, but still as if she should defend her intended. "He's a gentleman."

"I see." Flora sipped her tea, her eyes averted.

"He cares for me."

"Oh, yes, I've no doubt on the matter," Flora said, but her voice didn't mirror the words she spoke, something that embarrassed Penelope.

Was it possible to have a marriage without the ferocious passion she had felt with Drummond? Could she grow to have those same feelings with Theodore? Surely it was better to have a life built on proper understanding and shared standards.

Surely Penelope would be happier in a lovely townhouse with a polite husband who respected societal rules. Surely their marriage would be stronger by taking the traditional route of courtship and getting to know each other during proper dates instead of midnight rendezvous.

Surely….

Chapter Nineteen

Penelope added another sapphire pin into Flora's piled bun of curls, taking her time to dress the young woman. She was an indispensable wealth of diversion and amusement, something Penelope was in sore need of. Although she had only been back in London for a few days, Flora had been a perfect darling at keeping her mind busy with plans and gossip.

"Any more prodding and I'll look like a poodle." Flora laughed, touching a hand to the heaped hair upon her head.

"No, you look charming."

"Shouldn't *I* be primping and polishing *you*? It's your engagement dinner, after all."

Penelope picked up a pearl choker and fastened it around Flora's long neck, admiring her reflection in the mirror over the younger woman's shoulder. "Oh, posh. I've already found a husband. Now it's your turn."

"I do believe Conner would ride straight to London and kill any man who dare flirt with me."

"If you want to stay in London for good, a fine English gentleman is precisely what you need to plant you here. Your brother will come around soon enough to the fact that his sister is growing up."

Flora laughed. "I hope so."

"Come, now, we really must go down. My mother's been all a tizzy about this dinner for a week. If we aren't prompt, I fear she'll combust."

Penelope led the way from her bedroom down the hall and to the stairs. She lifted the hem of her pink silk gown carefully. Theodore had once said that the pale pink rose suited her well, and she bought her engagement dress specifically for his tastes. He was a good man and she would make an attempt to be worthy of him. As her mother always told her, a happily married man is a malleable man.

Flora peeked over the railing down at the ballroom below. "I'm certainly glad that Conner let me come back to London. This party looks amazing."

Penelope suddenly felt nervous for her grand debut as Theodore's future wife. She wondered if all the guests below could see the shame on her face or the invisible fingerprints Drummond left upon her skin. "Are there a lot of people?" she asked, her back against the wall.

"Loads. I see your parents by the landing. Are you ready to go down?"

"Yes, I suppose I must."

Flora turned with a gentle smile. "Don't fret, these people are all here out of love for you. They only want to see you happy. I'll go down and see you at the bottom, all right?"

"Let's go down together, yes?"

"If you're sure."

"Perfectly." Penelope wound her arm around Flora's.

As the pair made their appearance, the guests turned to watch. Almost all of society was there in their finery, glasses of champagne held in their gloved hands. She scanned the room for Theodore, spying him as a lone figure, pushing through the crowd and dodging a large floral display of pink and purple blossoms. He met her at the landing and held out a hand for her to take.

"You look marvelous," Theodore said as he took her hand. He pressed his lips to her knuckles, beaming as he looked back up at her.

"And you look very handsome," Penelope said honestly as Flora slipped from her side. "I do hope my mother hasn't completely harassed you?"

He chuckled and held out an arm for her to take. "She's been a perfect angel. I assure you she hasn't ran me off, just yet. I hope you might say the same after I introduce you to my parents."

"They've made it in time?" She was surprised. The Harrisons had been in Germany to take the fresh mountain air and, with such a swift engagement, they hardly had time to send out message of the party.

"Yes, and here they are." He held out his arm at an aging couple that seemed to appear out of nowhere. "Mother, Father, my future bride, Penelope. Penelope, these are my parents Gertrude and Kent."

"I'm very happy you could make it on such short

notice," Penelope said, smiling up at her future in-laws.

"And we're very happy that Theodore's finally settling down." Gertrude giggled good-naturedly, her white bun jiggling. Judging by the smell upon her breath, she had been partaking in celebratory drink, perhaps even to excess.

"Yes, yes." Kent nodded in agreement as he eyed his drunken wife. "We look forward to all the wedding festivities."

"Have you had the chance to meet my parents?" Penelope asked. "I know how pleased they were at the possibility of meeting you."

"Don't worry, when they arrived I made sure to bring them right over to meet your parents, as well as your brothers," Theodore assured her. "Now, we must go find our seats before the guests begin demanding their food."

Penelope allowed him to take her to one of the dozen tables that lined the ballroom. It had been set up for both dining and dancing, allowing for a long night. As they approached the seating, the rest of the guests began to take their places while Penelope and Theodore stood behind their chairs.

Her father rose from his seat beside Penelope, on the right. "Friends, relations, I am so pleased that you have all come to celebrate my only daughter's upcoming wedding. Mister Harrison—"

"Theodore, please!" he corrected with a grin. "We're family now!"

"*Theodore*," her father tipped his glass, "is the best son-in-law a man could hope for. I know he'll care for my Penelope as well as any father could dream and I welcome him into our family with open arms. To the happy couple."

"To the happy couple!" a chorus of voices replied, their cups raised.

"A few words, son?" Edmund asked, sitting down.

Theodore smiled down at Penelope before beginning. "When I first met Penelope at her birthday dinner, I knew she was to be my bride. Lovely, intelligent, witty and charming, she rivals any rose in regard to her outstanding beauty and impeccable personality. I count myself as the luckiest groom to have such a wonderful wife by my side."

Cecily let out a dramatic wail, her handkerchief completely soaked with happy tears.

Penelope was misty-eyed at Theodore's words and barely heard the guests as they applauded his speech. She was too busy gazing up at the wonderful man who wanted to take her to wife. But she was emotional for more reasons than just Theodore's little display. She felt guilty at all she had hidden from him, the late nights with Drummond and the secret love she bore him. Theodore deserved more and she needed to give it to him from that moment forward, with an open heart.

"Teddy, that was wonderful," Penelope whispered, clutching his arm as they sat.

His brows rose and his mouth split ear-to-ear. "Teddy, am I?"

"Unless you don't approve?" She silently chastised herself for being too forward. A nickname was a horrid idea, no matter how charming it sounded in her head.

"Quite the opposite," he said earnestly, bringing his face closer to hers. "I adore it."

Feeling pleased, she turned to her dinner, happier than she'd been in a while.

***

After her third straight twirl around the ballroom with Teddy, Penelope begged release. The heat of the crush and the tightness of her corset made it hard to catch her breath. She sat at the edge of the room while Teddy ran off to fetch her some refreshments.

"Darling party," Flora puffed as she plopped down in the seat beside Penelope and began wildly fanning herself. "I'm too full from supper for all this dancing."

"So you're having fun?" she asked with a smile.

"Too much, I'm afraid."

Penelope frowned and began adjusting the pins in Flora's hair. Loose golden tendrils were rapidly making their escape. "It shows."

"Your parents seem to have invited everyone in the city."

"And then some." Penelope scanned the guests, spying a number of familiar faces. "I see quite a few of my brother's friends have come in from the country."

Flora straightened up in her chair, immediately snapping her fan shut. "Any eligible bachelors worth noting?"

"If I say yes, I fear your brother will throttle me!" She laughed, looking through the masses for Teddy and her drink.

"Please, Penelope." Flora clasped her hands together, her eyes still upon the guests. "Introduce me to some eligible bachelors. *You've* found a proper man, now it's my turn! You've said it yourself. If I can find a husband, then I would have cause to stay in London. I think I would make a bonny little wife."

"You're trying very hard to look innocent, but I see that MacLeod glint in your eye."

"I have no idea what you're talking about," Flora sniffed, but her lips curled upward.

"Fine, just a few of the nicer ones, and no one I've been involved with. My mother would never allow it due to all of their invisible flaws."

"Oh, goody!" She jumped up, pulling Penelope with her. "So, who's first?"

Penelope looked around and spotted her first target. She promptly led Flora to a tall, thin, man with a mop of blond hair and freckled cheeks. "Henry, may I introduce you to my friend Flora MacLeod? Flora, this is Henry Gettings, Baron Gettings' youngest son."

"How do you do?" Henry bowed over Flora's hand.

"Lovely to meet you," she replied, pinking as he squared his broad shoulders.

"May I request a place on your dance card, Miss?" Henry asked.

"Certainly!" Flora flipped the booklet open. "Three dances from now?"

"My pleasure."

Henry melted back into the crowd and, as soon he was out of earshot, Penelope whispered into Flora's ear, "What do you think of him?"

"He's very handsome. But with the light hair, he reminds me of Conner."

"Really?" Penelope pictured Charlotte's husband and frowned. "They're nothing alike."

"Next."

Penelope sighed and made a beeline toward the next man—a bit bookish and quiet, but a jolly fellow her brother held in high esteem. "Andrew!"

A slim gentleman looked up from his cup, startled. "Oh, Penelope, congratulations."

"Andrew, I'd like to introduce you to Flora MacLeod." Penelope gestured toward her friend. "Flora, this is Andrew Philips. He went to school with my middle brother."

"Lovely to meet you," Flora said.

Andrew blushed deeply, clearing his throat several times. "N-nice to meet you."

Penelope struggled to keep her face placid. "Andrew, Flora has a few slots still open on her dance card."

His eyes widened. "Oh…ye-yes, um, Miss MacLeod, c-can…may I have the pleasure of a dance?"

Flora nodded and opened her book, making a small note. "I have you down for the next waltz, if that would be agreeable?"

His lips pursed as he agreed. "Y-yes, very."

"Lovely to see you," Penelope said as she steered Flora away.

"Does he have a stutter?" Flora asked in a whisper.

"No, I think he's just nervous. He's a shy fellow, but darling, once he opens up."

"Ooh, who's that?" Penelope nodded toward a red-haired man who emptied a glass of champagne in one swallow.

Penelope was about to make the introductions when Teddy popped up by her side, two glasses in hand. "Ladies, I've been on quite a chase trying to find you."

"So sorry, I was taking Flora around to meet everyone," Penelope told him as she gratefully sipped her drink.

Flora took the other cup. "Penelope is going to try to introduce me to some nice men."

"Well, have you met my brother?" Teddy asked eagerly. "Franklin's a true gentleman."

Flora raised her brows and grinned at Penelope. "No, I haven't."

"Then, please, allow me to take you." Teddy held out an arm. "Penelope, is it all right?"

"Certainly!"

Penelope watched as the pair darted toward where Franklin sat with Edmund. While Franklin was nice enough, she couldn't imagine Flora happy with him. Flora seemed to love a rogue, if Charlotte's explanation of her beau back in Scotland was any indication of that. Franklin was an enthusiastic chap, but certainly not Flora's taste. Although, she did appreciate Teddy's suggestion, as she knew he did it out of the goodness of his heart.

Yes, Teddy was a fine man, better than she ever

deserved. He was kind, considerate, and all too charming. She had no doubt that he would be the perfect husband and she would work hard to be the perfect wife.

Chapter Twenty

The next morning Penelope languished in bed, spending much of her breakfast opening notes from well-wishers over her tray of scones and clotted cream. Everyone who was anyone dropped off their calling cards for the future married couple and Penelope was left to sift through them. She had thought about doing it with Teddy, as she didn't know who half of the writers were, but thought better of it, as she would soon need to know all of those faceless names by heart.

A light knock on her bedroom door jarred her from her tea and Flora flew in, all ruffles and lace, her hair streaming down her face. If it were any other girl, her appearance would have been shocking. But, since it was the young Scotswoman, Penelope was hardly surprised.

"Well, good morning," Penelope laughed, setting down her teacup. "If I knew you were coming, I would have been better prepared."

"Don't bother prettying up on my account," Flora said as she sat on the edge of the bed and picked up a scone. “I just stopped by.”

“What are you up to today?”

Flora finished chewing before answering. “Well, as you know, your fiancé introduced me to his brother Franklin, who begged a walk in the gardens this afternoon.”

“That should be nice. The weather is very agreeable.”

“Could you and Theodore come with us?”

Penelope groaned. “I was up ever so late last night. Can’t you just bring a chaperone?”

“You know I’d never bring a chaperone. The idea of that old maid Conner sent to trail me following about and tittering isn’t my idea of a pleasant outing.” Flora laughed. “To be honest, I’m not really…the elder Mister Harrison is…”

“Not your type?” Penelope asked, moving her tray off her lap.

Flora let out a long sigh and shook her head. “Not at all. I just didn’t know how to say no without offending either of the Harrison brothers.”

“Don’t fret, you don’t have to marry Franklin,” she assured her with a gentle pat on the leg. “Would it really make you feel better if I were to accompany you?”

“Please do!”

“I suppose I should send a note to Teddy about accompanying us,” Penelope thought aloud as she prepared to rise from bed.

“Oh, don’t bother,” Flora told her, snatching another scone from the plate. “I’ve taken the liberty of sending out a note with a maid before I came up.”

"Did you now? What if I had said no?"

Flora cocked her head to the side. "Would you have?"

"Hardly." She swung her legs to the floor and stretched her arms. Her fingers were tight from hours of mindless note writing. "Will you help me dress? Then I can arrange your hair."

"That's why I'm here."

Penelope pulled a violet silk from her dresser and, after tightening a corset around her waist, Flora helped her to button the back. Together they worked as a well-oiled machine, one tightening stays and fastening jewels while the other coiled hair and pinned a wide-brimmed hat. Penelope was rightly pleased when they were both primped and primed for a jaunt through the gardens.

With a glance at a grandfather clock that stood between two windows, Flora nodded pertly. "I suppose it's time to descend. I told them they could collect us around noon."

"You're certainly lucky I agreed. Otherwise, you would have had a rather awkward carriage ride."

Flora giggled and followed Penelope down the stairs, moving with the grace of carefree youth that Penelope felt she had left long behind. How jolly and nimble Flora looked as she trailed behind, not even bothering to lift the hem of her gown from the floor. For a moment, despite the difference in complexions and coloring, she reminded Penelope of Charlotte, and the thought tugged at her chest as she wished her friend were back in London, telling Penelope to follow her heart. Perhaps, then, she would listen.

Penelope shook the thought from her head and straightened her spine, feeling her engagement ring tighten upon her finger. Teddy was a dear, a true gentleman, and Penelope would do better to remember the fact. When they got to the bottom of the stairs, she almost collided with a butler, who was just on his way to fetch the girls.

"Miss Elmsly, Lady MacLeod, the two Mister Harrisons are here," he said with a slight bow.

Penelope looked over his shoulder to Teddy and Franklin, who were completely visible next to the front door. "Thank you."

"Penelope." Teddy grinned widely, holding out pink roses. "I would have brought something more exotic, had I known you would be gracing me with your presence today. An exceedingly marvelous treat."

"I do love roses. Thank you, Teddy." She allowed him to kiss her hand, then delicately sniffed the blooms before passing them off to the butler.

"Lady MacLeod, a pleasure." Franklin shot her a toothy smile and his cheeks pinked when she nodded back to him. Penelope could tell that the poor lad was smitten with the sprightly wood nymph.

"Mr. Harrison, good afternoon. Please, call me Flora."

Penelope pursed her lips. She didn't think it proper for Flora to have Franklin address her so commonly, but knew better than to tell her so. Every time she did something of the sort, she was told it was merely the Scottish way. Still, since Flora wasn't interested in perusing him further, it was almost giving the unfortunate chap false hope. Shame.

She sat in the back of the open carriage beside Flora, the men in the front. The ride to Kensington gardens was pleasant enough. The men spoke aloud about the newest operas while Flora gushed openly of her love for the theater. Every so often, Teddy would look over his shoulder at Penelope, giving her a warm look that softened her with each glance. When they finally reached the gardens, he helped her from the carriage, holding her hand for longer than was proper.

"You look delightful today," Teddy whispered beneath the brim of her hat as she straightened her skirts.

"Thank you, Teddy."

He smiled at her and held out his elbow for her to take. For a moment, she had thought he might kiss her, something that other engaged couples might do. She longed to see if a spark was ignited when their lips met for the first time. She wondered if his kisses would be full of desire and passion, or gentle and timid. Would he cup her face with his hand when they embraced? Would his fingers pull the pins from her hair to see how it shone in the sunlight? Would he moan with need, or mutter nothings into her ear?

"Are you well, Penelope?" Teddy asked, looking down at her with a slight frown. "You look rather dazed."

She bit her lip and glanced over to Flora and Franklin, who were inspecting a rather large fountain. She wanted to know—*needed* to know—

what their kiss would feel like.

"Teddy, I do hope you don't think me forward," she began quietly, pulling him over to a bench, which was slightly hidden behind a rosebush, but not so hidden as to be lewd.

He chuckled and patted her hand. "My dear, you say that so often, but you're never forward. You're always the picture of feminine propriety."

While the words should flatter her, she almost wished he would throw propriety to the wind and show her how he felt. She briefly thought about how shameful her thoughts were. But her need to know their true passion overwhelmed her thoughts.

"Teddy, I want you to kiss me," she told him in a hushed tone, her eyes trained carefully on his.

Taken aback, he cleared his throat, his brows drifting upward toward his perfectly coifed hair. "Pardon?"

Penelope felt her cheeks warm. She didn't expect him to react so. Well, she didn't know exactly what she should have expected. "I want you to kiss me," she repeated carefully.

Teddy twisted his head about him, seemingly looking for anyone who may be watching, before turning back to her. "Well, I suppose we *are* engaged." He licked his lips thoughtfully then the corners lifted.

He took both her hands and pulled her closer, tentatively bringing his mouth to hers. His jaw was smooth, but his lips were oddly dry and stayed sealed for the entirety of their ridiculously chaste kiss. Penelope felt her stomach churn, as she was reminded of kissing her great aunt Elizabeth, who was so elderly that her skin felt like worn parchment. She hadn't expected passionate sparks, not exactly, but she had expected *something*. Something other than disgust.

"Oh, Penelope," he muttered into her mouth as he pulled away from their brief embrace. "I am so glad we had that moment. How terribly naughty of us." His brown eyes twinkled with mirth. "Now we have our very own secret."

Penelope forced herself to smile. Surely that one kiss wasn't the only one they would share in their lifetime together. There would be passion and desire after they were wed, surely. Perhaps he was merely nervous—a new lover who didn't know how to hold a woman. Or maybe he was frightened of a passerby catching them in the act. Yes, that was it. She was sure the next one would be better, more romantic and full of the deep feeling she hadn't felt since—

"There you two lovebirds are!" Franklin's head popped over the top of the hedge, all teeth and bug eyes, a most peculiar looking bird.

Teddy stood up quickly, his face red. "Just sitting a moment, no need to fuss."

"Lady MacLeod has taken too much sun, I'm afraid," Franklin told them seriously. "I thought we should take the ladies home to rest."

Penelope looked over at Flora, who gave her a sharp wink.

Teddy helped her to stand and nodded. "The sun is rather strong today. It may be for the best that we don't overexert ourselves. Must be in tiptop shape for the wedding, after all."

Once they were all safely deposited in the

carriage, Flora placed her hand upon Penelope's knee and squeezed her leg, shooting her a knowing glance. Penelope's chest and neck heated for the second time that day and she turned her head away, grateful for her friend's understanding, but also embarrassed that her discomfort with Teddy was so apparent.

She tried concentrating on the horses they passed, counting the tall bays and dappled greys. But then Flora began to chatter beside her, telling her all about the summer storms in Scotland with thunder so loud it would shake the glass, but with rain so soft one could stand beneath the water, not caring how soaked they became. Penelope closed her eyes as she imagined the shower, cool and sweet, washing over her face, sating the thirst of green Scottish hills. She pictured the tallest mount, covered in small purple blooms, where a lone figure stood, beckoning her home.

Chapter Twenty-One

Penelope was let into the Harrison mansion by a prim butler in perfectly pressed livery. She felt a delicious chill up her spine as she stepped into the threshold. She could scarcely believe that in two weeks time, this grand house would become her home, the home where she would build a life with Teddy. He was a kind man, thoughtful, and while not particularly passionate, he was a steady match who did his best to ensure she was treated with the utmost care.

The butler bowed as she entered. "Master Harrison is in the drawing room. Shall I escort you?"

"Don't worry yourself." Penelope patted her feathered hat. She had bought it to match Teddy's favorite shade of pink on her. "I know where it is."

She strolled down a long hallway, turning at the end to reach the drawing room door. She straightened her skirts before knocking, but heard no answer. Normally, she would never surprise him so, but just the day before he told her to stop by her future home more often. Perhaps he wished to redo their secret kiss to add more passion to their lives.

Assuming he was hard at his work, she entered quietly, so as to disturb him as little at possible. However, what she found in that cozy study was more than she could bear.

Her fiancé stood in a passionate embrace with a young, rail-thin woman in a maid's uniform. His jacket had been tossed to the floor alongside a discarded apron and Penelope felt herself grow physically ill as she watched her betrothed begin a careful undressing of the hired help. The comfort between the two hinted that they had done this before. He certainly didn't kiss Penelope the way he kissed the maid.

Throwing her head back in unbridled delight, the maid noticed her in the doorway and let out a shrill shriek.

Theodore whipped around, mouth agape as his gaze settled on her. "Penelope," he said, slowing dropping his arms from around the maid's waist. "How…how long have you been there?"

"Long enough," she hissed as the maid scurried out of the room in fear, her apron clutched to her bare chest. "What is the meaning of this?"

Theodore cleared his throat and straightened his necktie, his hair a tousled mess. "I'm very sorry you had to witness that."

"You're *very sorry*?" Penelope repeated in disbelief. "I find you groping that girl less than two weeks before our wedding and that's all you have to say to me?"

A look of pure confusion crossed his face.

"You're cross with me?"

"Of course I am!" she cried, feeling hot tears of frustration wash down her cheeks. Her blatant display of emotion humiliated her all the more. "Why wouldn't I be?"

Sighing, Theodore crossed to her, taking her in his arms and gently patting her back. She cringed when she smelled the scent of freshly baked bread and wood smoke on his lapel. Since he wasn't one to bake his own rolls, Penelope knew the smell came from the maid.

"I am very sorry, my dear," he crooned, as if speaking to an unstable person. "I know that was terribly unseemly and I promise you won't have to be witness to my activities in the future."

Penelope pulled back in disgust. "Teddy, correct me if I am mistaken, but that didn't sound much like a promise that you'll never commit adultery, merely that I won't *see* it."

"Well, yes. I swear that I will be more considerate in the future." He smiled down at her as if he were being particularly reasonable.

Her mouth flapped uncommonly like a fish out of water, searching for air as she now searched for answers. "This is terrible. You're admitting that you're going to step outside of our marriage bed."

"Penelope, darling, I—"

"Don't you 'Penelope, darling' me!" She roughly brushed the wetness from her cheek. "You've made a fool of me, Teddy, and I don't think I can forgive it."

"What are you saying, Penelope?"

"I'm saying that I can't marry you. I can't tie

myself to a man who would toss aside his vows and amuse himself with the maids."

Theodore leaned back against his desk and rubbed his temples tiredly. "You don't mean that."

"I do," she whispered, slowly pulling the engagement ring from her hand. "Goodbye, Teddy." Penelope placed the ring upon his desk and hurried from the room. She wished, vaguely, that she would hear the stomp of footsteps, his voice calling her name, a vow of fidelity and love. But it never came.

***

"You *what*?" Cecily squawked, falling at once onto a settee. "I can't believe it. I *won't* believe it!"

"It's true. He's been involving himself in inappropriate relationships and has told me he plans to continue them, albeit more discreetly. Perhaps not with the same maid, but that doesn't matter."

Cecily moaned and called out to the butler for some smelling salts. "Penelope, oh, Penelope, what have you done?"

"What I needed to do." She took a seat at her mother's feet, slowly unpinning her hat. She had a terrible headache.

"My dear, sweet daughter. This is all just a…a terrible misunderstanding. Yes, that's it. A small lover's quarrel."

"This isn't just cold feet over the wedding, this is blatant adultery."

"Perhaps you saw it wrong?" Cecily suggested thoughtfully. "Could it be that he was…that she was, maybe, helping him to dress? Or she had something in her eye?"

Penelope shook her head. "I don't believe so. I saw it all with my own eyes. It was undoubtedly clear that they were engaging in some unseemly behavior."

"You're so young. So new." Cecily rose gingerly and took her hands. "Marriage is complicated and we all have special roles to play. The men provide for their families and act as the head of the household. And the women run the home, bear the children, and turn their heads when the situation calls for it. Surely, you may do that as so many others have."

She gasped, her stomach dropping. "Turn a blind eye to his indiscretions? I can't believe you'd want that for me."

"Penelope, this is the way of men. They will stray, have their fun, and return home to us in time for tea."

"*Us*?" She croaked, pulling her fingers from her mother's grasp. "Is that was my father does? He runs around with the maids and you ignore it?" She flipped through the list of Elmsly maids in her mind, feeling sicker as she imagined each with her father.

Cecily pursed her lips. "He has been a good husband and I, a good wife. Theodore could be a good husband to you, if you let him."

"I don't believe I could share my husband with other women like that."

"Then you will end up very much alone," Cecily said evenly, if not a bit sadly.

"That can't be true. Charlotte's husband is

exceedingly faithful to her. They are hardly ever apart."

Cecily scoffed. "Is that what you believe? He must go sow his wild Scottish oats just as the rest of the men do. It's in their very nature."

Penelope stood, preparing to go up to her rooms. "I don't care what you have to say about it. There are no justifications for his behavior and I won't go through with this wedding."

"You must!" Cecily shot up, grabbing her arm and pulling her around. "Penelope, your father and I have tried to shield you from the many realities of this world, but it is time you knew what's really going on."

"What are you talking about?"

"The arcade is failing, darling. People import things directly from France now."

Penelope paled. The shopping center was her father's life's work. "It can't be."

"It is. We've gone through our funds trying to keep it afloat, but I'm afraid the business will close soon."

"*All* of the funds? You mean there's nothing more?"

Cecily nodded, her eyes welling up with tears. "The money's *gone*. We've saved for your dowry, and enough for a wedding, but aside from that, we are practically impoverished."

All of the pieces clicked together. "Is this why you're pushing me to reconcile with Teddy?"

"One of the many reasons, yes. I am being truthful when I say that he'll be a good husband to you, as well as having the funds and exotic products to save the Piccadilly Emporium."

Penelope felt her mouth go dry. "Oh, Mother, I had no idea."

"We won't force you to marry Theodore. I would never expect you to enter into a marriage with a man you do not love. I'm just asking you to consider your options and find it in your heart to forgive him if you can."

"I-I must go lie down," Penelope choked out, her mind spinning wildly. "I must have time alone to think."

She staggered up the stairs of her childhood home, passing the paintings of her distant relations—men in military garb, women surrounded by gaggles of children, couples seated in front of the very fireplace downstairs in the library. Penelope couldn't bear the thought of those portraits being sold to pay the rent. It seemed such a silly thing to her, to worry so about some pictures she had never paid any attention to before. But the notion that they could soon be hung in the houses of other people, people tittering about the fate of the poor Elmsly family, almost brought her to her knees.

Once she was safely in her bedroom, the door locked, she went to her writing desk and pulled out a sheet of fine paper, preparing to write. If a marriage to Theodore was what it took to keep her family afloat, Penelope knew what was to be done.

Chapter Twenty-Two

When Penelope awoke the next morning, she stretched in bed, staring up at the canopy above her. For a brief moment, she had forgotten the humiliating display of the previous day, but as soon as she saw her crumpled gown upon the floor and the dinner tray beside it, she instantly felt ill.

After she'd left her mother, Penelope had locked herself into her room, refusing her parents' pleas for entry. She had only let a maid slip her a tray of food which was largely untouched. The mere thought of eating churned her stomach.

Sliding out of bed, she threw open her bedroom window and looked out onto the road. Carriages passed, couples walked, and love continued on her block while she felt positively trapped inside. It was nearly noon and she would be expected to leave her quarters at some point that day, something she certainly wasn't looking forward to.

She leaned against the window frame, reflecting on the great weight set upon her. When Cecily had revealed that the Elmsly family was practically impoverished, Penelope couldn't believe it. There had been no change in their lifestyle; they still had a team of maids, her father never complained when a new dress from Paris arrived, and the engagement party had been impeccably designed and executed with fine wine and delicacies. But now the Piccadilly Emporium was in jeopardy and only Penelope's marriage to Theodore had any hopes of saving it.

Sighing, she called for a maid to help her dress. She could guess that Theodore would make an appearance at some point that day and Penelope needed to be prepared. While he did not have the same things to lose by a failed engagement, people would certainly gossip and speculate as to why the beautiful Elmsly girl had ended the marriage plans. Such chatter, still, was never good for a businessman.

Once she was dressed in a deep blue velvet day gown with her hair styled beneath a ribbon-topped hat, she took a deep breath and descended down to lunch. Her parents looked up from their soup, stunned as she calmly sat at her place at the table. She primly laid her napkin upon her lap, thanking the butler as he served her.

Edmund looked nervously from his wife to his daughter. "Good day, Penelope."

"Good day," she answered evenly, sipping her soup. Usually one of her favorite dishes, the flavorful broth seemed to taste sour and thin.

"And how are you feeling?" Edmund asked carefully.

Penelope looked up with a smile that didn't quite

reach her eyes. "Perfectly well, thank you. I am just waiting for my scoundrel of a fiancé to come grovel so I can take him back, becoming a dutiful wife, thus saving the arcade from closure and the family from financial ruin." She ate another spoonful of soup.

Cecily and Edmund stared at each other with wide eyes. Penelope's mother took Edmund's hand and cleared her throat. "Darling, we can't begin to—"

Penelope held up a hand. "Don't. I'm doing this for the good of the family and I don't wish to speak of it again. Ever."

"Pardon me, Miss Elmsly," the butler whispered. "I have several deliveries if you would like to receive them?"

"Just on schedule," Penelope said, placing her spoon upon the table. She sighed, knowing just what she would expect. "I will receive them now."

The butler offered her a silver tray with a letter. "The footmen will bring in the items presently."

Penelope slid open the envelope with her butter knife, unfolding the paper carefully to reveal Theodore's practiced hand.

My darling Penelope,

What occurred yesterday is now among my greatest regrets in life because it hurt you. Your feelings and well-being are some of my top priorities and I cannot live knowing that you feel so badly.

Please accept these gifts as a sincere apology until I may call upon you this afternoon to ask for your forgiveness in person.

Dearest regards,

Theodore Harrison

"How romantic," she mumbled, roughly shoving the letter back into the envelope.

"Is it from Theodore?" Cecily questioned eagerly.

"Obviously." She watched as several footmen entered carrying a massive arrangement of colorful bird of paradise flowers. Another footman came with three hatboxes and the last offered her a fur stole.

Cecily rose, inspecting each gift with satisfied nods until she reached the flowers. "What interesting blooms."

"Birds of paradise," Edmund said. "Quite exotic."

A short burst of laughter escaped Penelope's lips. "If I recall Theodore's books correctly, they mean faithfulness and loyalty. How hilariously ironic."

"He's trying his best," Cecily cooed.

"The hats, I'll take," she said, rising from her seat and taking the boxes. "Get rid of the flowers and send the fur to someone who might have use for it."

Without waiting for further parental

involvement, Penelope left to go to her room. She opened the hatboxes and inspected each finery within. Theodore knew of her fondness for hats and was abusing that knowledge spectacularly. Pausing to shove the hatboxes into her accessory wardrobe, Penelope sat down at her writing desk.

Taking a breath, she pulled a tiny key from one drawer and used it to open a small compartment. From it she pulled out the ring given to her by Drummond MacLeod. She had kept the ring, a gold band with a row of amethysts and diamonds, hidden away since the day of the engagement to Theodore.

Hands shaking, she slid the jewelry onto her right ring finger. She stifled what might have been a sob, silently cursing herself for the uninvited emotions. Penelope could scarcely say what led her to put on Drummond's ring. She did so almost mechanically, without thought. Once he had returned to Scotland, and Theodore made his intentions clear, she had promised herself she would never think of Drummond again.

But she did think of him. She thought of his bright-eyed intensity, the way he studied both her and the music she wrote for him. She thought of how he scanned each room as he entered, almost always finding her in a crowd. She thought of the heat of his palm upon her cheek as they parted and the final kiss he placed upon her ringed hand. She thought of him always, almost more than she should.

She had resigned herself to a life as Theodore Harrison's wife, to be his true partner in all things until her dying day, and then on into the afterlife for eternity. She had made herself a prison in in the gilded cage she worked hard to build. But at each turn, she was beaten down, as a little bird would be without enough room to stretch her wings. Penelope had given up love and passion for a lifetime of marriage to a man who would constantly turn his back on her, no matter how hard she tried to please him. What she once longed for had become spoiled and now she had no choice but to play the part.

The tears flowed openly now, dripping into the velvet of her dress and making her pale skin unattractively blotchy. The more she reflected on the true and pure love she could have had, the harder she cried. Sobs were healing, in a way, cleansing her soul of the feelings she suppressed for so many weeks.

"Penelope?" Her mother's voice jarred her from her emotional state.

Penelope cleared her throat, trying to keep her voice steady. "What is it?"

"Theodore's here, darling. He wants to talk to you. Please come down."

"In a moment." She got up from her desk and walked into her bathroom, groaning as she saw her face in the mirror. Mottled and bloated from tears, she could hardly face Theodore like that. She splashed cold water on her face for several moments then stopped at her dressing table to powder her nose. Her eyes were still red-rimmed but she no longer looked completely ravaged by tears. The poor sod would probably think she cried for *him*. The senseless cad.

Penelope took her time walking downstairs,

prepping herself to see Theodore again. While she wasn't passionately in love with him, she had been prepared to be his wife and devote herself to him. Seeing him with his hands all over that maid had broken her heart. She pardoned herself the selfish feeling as she reached the landing, feeling the heat of anger swelling within her core.

Theodore was in the study waiting for her, a bouquet of purple hyacinth in his hands. "Penelope, I am so pleased you agreed to see me."

"Theodore," she greeted, sitting alone on an armchair. Usually she would sit upon the couch to see him, allowing him a place beside her, but today she was less than interested in his closeness.

He fell to his knees next to the lounger, clasping the flowers in one hand, the other placed dramatically over his heart. "Penelope, please don't be cross with me. One indiscretion means *nothing* in the grand scheme of life. We're a perfectly matched pair of looks, breeding, societal standing. You and I are simply meant to be."

Penelope sighed, daring to look into his eager face. "You've hurt me, Theodore."

"Theodore? I have been demoted from Teddy to Theodore? Is there no hope for reconciliation?"

"I can't feel like this every day of our marriage. I won't stand for it. I can't pause before every door, frightened that you'll be…that you would…with a maid."

"And you won't have to. The maids are all gone." He paused. "Well, except for old Miss Wilma, but she's certainly not the spring chicken you would have to fear." When Penelope didn't laugh along with him, he frowned. "Please stop all this, Penelope. Accept my apology so we might be married."

Penelope bit her lip. While she wanted nothing more than to beat him upon the head with those violet blooms, she knew she had a duty to her family. "I will forgive you, Theodore, but it will take time for me to heal from this."

"Of course." He took her hand, kissing it roughly. "I won't disappoint you again. We will live a fine life, Penelope. I am *so* fond of you."

She smiled wryly as he prattled on about what *fine* trips they would take and what *fine* children they would have. And she thought how it was *not* at all fine to have a husband who was merely *fond* of her.

Chapter Twenty-Three

"Penelope, darling, you're a perfect angel!" Cecily gushed, adjusting the hem of her daughter's bridal veil. "Theodore is the luckiest of men."

"If only he acted so," she muttered, looping a strand of pearls around her slender neck.

"Don't be cross," her mother scolded, wagging a finger. "It's your wedding day and a sour bride makes for a sour marriage.

Penelope was about to remark that sleeping with the help also made for a particularly sour marriage, but thought better of goading her. She knew that going through with the wedding was necessary, but couldn't bring herself to plaster more than the merest of smiles on her face. Anything else would be more than exhausting.

Theodore had been the utmost gentleman since she caught him in a rather distasteful position with the young maid. Every spare hour he had was dedicated to taking her to dinner and showering her with lavish gifts that sat largely unopened in the corner of her room, and generally doting upon her in ostentatious ways. But it did little to ease her mind about the philandering she was sure would occur once they were wed. The fact that she would soon spend her days eyeing every woman Theodore looked twice at already tired her.

She had pictured her wedding day so differently in her innocent youth, and even more so when Theodore first gave her his attentions so many months ago. Penelope had thought she'd be a blushing bride to a proud groom who only had eyes for her. And while she had resigned herself to a marriage to a man she wouldn't truly love, she hated that she would also be tied to a husband that would shame her with his whores. Yes, her wedding day felt more like a funeral without the guarantee of a beautiful heaven afterward.

"We must go now, dear, or we'll be late." Cecily was bursting with excitement, flitting around Penelope's bedroom, packing last minute things for her honeymoon.

Penelope nodded and glanced at the piles of trunks and bags that waited their departure for their honeymoon. She then followed her mother down the stairs to where her father waited in the foyer. With each step she felt her heart grow at heavy as her massive wedding dress.

"A vision," Edmund declared, looking dapper in a new suit.

"Thank you, Father." Penelope allowed him to help her into the carriage, followed by her mother. She tried fixing her face to look more positive about the day's festivities, but she found she couldn't muster a single positive thought.

Penelope leaned against the side of the carriage, tuning out her parents' excited tittering about the wedding and the rich son they would soon receive. She was pleased the family's store would be saved, as Theodore had promised a hefty sum for its bills, but rather felt as if she were being sold, something she wouldn't have minded a year ago. However, now things were different. *She* was different. She knew what love and devotion felt like and it pained her greatly to be signing those feelings away forever.

The roads were clogged with carriages, as they usually were on Sunday mornings. They should have left earlier for the church, but she liked that the traffic bought her some extra time as a free woman. As far as the carriages went, Penelope was pleased. It gave her something to focus on as they sat in the late summer heat. She opened a window a crack, letting in fresh air. It smelled like rain and the storm clouds above mimicked the tempest that swelled within her heart. Most of the people she spied carried umbrellas for the later rains that were sure to come. She tried to remember if rain was good luck for a wedding but then decided that it didn't really matter. Her nuptials were already cursed.

A little girl ran up to the side of the carriage, noticing the orange blossoms upon it, signifying that a bride was inside. They waved to each other and the child's eagerness to catch a glimpse of her thawed her heart a bit. Her round face and gap-toothed smile was adorable, and although Penelope hated to think of it, she wondered what kind of man the child would later meet. Would she marry a strong and brave man who made her heart sing? Or would she find herself with a rich philanderer? The girl's mother smiled and held a hand to her heart as if to say, "I remember when it was my time," before pulling her daughter back into the crowd.

Among the throngs of busting people, one stood out that made Penelope's blood run cold in her veins. A head taller than the rest stood Drummond, waiting to cross the lanes, a package tucked under his arm. He didn't see her—something Penelope wasn't sure should make her glad, or not. His emerald eyes scanned the crowds calmly, glazing right over her carriage. Penelope longed to call out to him or leap from her seat, but knew she couldn't.

She kept her eyes upon him until he was lost in the swarm. Penelope had no idea if he truly *was* in London. It could have been anyone…in a kilt…with green eyes…on the same boulevard as the MacLeod townhouse. Yes, anyone. Well, if Flora knew, she certainly didn't tell her. Instead of wondering, she tried to commit him to memory. It wasn't hard, as she had memorized each curve and line of his face during their nights together. She closed her eyes, almost thankful that she would always remember him as young and healthy, a handsome specimen who could never be trumped.

"Penelope, are you well?" Cecily asked. "You look as if you've seen a ghost!"

"Because I have."

***

Once Cecily left for her seat, and the only people

not in the pews were Penelope and her father, she allowed herself a moment of panic. The church was packed with wedding guests and the groom stood beside the altar, waiting to receive his bride. She recalled being there for Charlotte's wedding and lamented how different the event had felt. The love in the room was palpable and no one could deny how devoted the couple was to one another. Penelope wished she could have that simple luxury. She feared her distaste would be evident upon her face and the guests would all see that she basically a hostage in the church.

Thunder clapped outside and lightning flashed violently, sending bursts of light through the stained glass of the dressing room she was now cloistered in. Her father paced, grumbling about the shoddy weather and how he hoped it wouldn't deter the guests from joining them for the pricey reception. She knew he had spent the last of the Elmsly money on the after party.

Penelope took deep breaths as the room spun, craving Drummond's strong presence to ground her. The fact that he was in London startled her, even scared her in a way. She thought he was lost to her forever and, yet, there he was. She had almost hoped that she had been mistaken and mixed him up with another man, but she knew it was impossible. She knew him too well.

Did he know she was getting married at that moment? Penelope wasn't sure. Certainly Flora had told him, since it was assumed he would be at the MacLeod townhouse. She picked at the flowers in her bouquet, dreading the moment she had to walk down the aisle. She would much rather run into Drummond's arms and leave the pressures behind.

At that moment, Penelope knew what had to be done. She loved Drummond, loved him desperately and without measure. She would rather be the poor wife of a Scottish warrior than the rich wife of a British philanderer and she had to do everything in her power to make that a reality, no matter the cost.

She paused, glancing at her father who stood by the window, watching the storm. How she would hate to disappoint him.

"Father." Penelope's voice was small. "Father, I need to say something."

"What is it, dear? Ready to make your grand entrance?"

She put down her bouquet and took a deep breath. "No. I'm not going."

"What was that?" Edmund knitted his brows.

"I'm not marrying Theodore. I can't."

Edmund sputtered. "But-but you must. It's your wedding day! Everyone's waiting for you."

Penelope fisted her hands, trying to quell the shaking. "I can't. I don't love him."

"What has love got to do with a marriage? You merely have a case of cold feet. Nothing a good set of vows can't fix." He chuckled at his own joke.

"I'm in love with someone else. I have been for some time, but I was afraid we'd lose the arcade and I didn't know what to do."

Edmund's face fell. "What did you say?"

"I'm in love with Drummond MacGregor but he doesn't think he deserves me and he left some time ago, back to Scotland. I settled myself for Theodore until I caught him with a maid. I thought about writing to Drummond and running away with him, but Mother told me that he was the only chance to save the family."

"Is that why you're marrying him? For the…the money?" Edmund almost whispered the question.

"Yes." Penelope's voice wavered and she felt her knees grow weak as she spoke. "I would have never let things go this far, otherwise. But I couldn't let you lose the arcade."

"Oh, God, I've ruined everything." Her father put his head in his hands. "Penelope, I would have never asked you to sacrifice yourself for the arcade. I wouldn't want that for you."

"I know, but I felt that I had to. But now I need to leave before it's too late."

Edmund glanced up at her and nodded slowly. "I understand."

Penelope was almost aghast at his serenity. Was it the calmness before the storm? "Do you?"

"I do." He drew closer and folded her into his arms.

Penelope hadn't noticed how frail her father had become. She knew he was getting older, as was life, but didn't realize how brittle he felt. She feared her leaving the wedding would send him over the edge, but he seemed at peace as he hugged her tightly.

"Now what?" she dared to ask, as they pulled apart. "What do we do?"

"About what? The hoards of people waiting for you to make your grand entrance?" He smiled wryly, probably pondering the same thing.

"I suppose I'll have to go and explain myself."

"No." Edmund sighed. "I'll take care of everything. Don't fret."

"You don't have to do that. I must clean up my own mess and explain myself to everyone."

"This isn't your mess, Penelope. You should have never been dragged into my financial affairs. I'll deal with everything."

"Father, I don't know what to say."

He patted her cheek fondly. "Then say nothing, and go."

Penelope nodded and turned to leave before remembering something. She pulled Theodore's ring from her finger and passed it to her father. Without the cursed stone weighing her down, Penelope's fear was gone, replaced by a new tranquility she hadn't felt for some time.

Before she lost her nerve, she dashed through the empty hall and out to where the carriage dropped them off an hour earlier. But, the road was heartbreakingly empty. She peered around the edge of the building, careful to stay under the refectory's eaves. Never in her life had she not had a carriage at her instant disposal and, now, there were none to be had. Soon the guests would be released from the failed ceremony and Penelope would rather die than be caught skulking about the church grounds to feel the full force of society's judgment.

Thunder clapped loudly, making her jump. Rain pelted the ground and Penelope tried to recall the route to the MacLeod house. It wasn't more than three streets to the east, and she thought she could make it in a few minutes if she ran fast enough.

Penelope picked up the hem of her heavy dress

and took a final, deep breath and raced into the rain, almost laughing from both glee and embarrassment. As the water fell, her skirts soaked in the wet, making the silks even heavier than before. She struggled to keep them up as she ran and nearly burst out in laughter as she imagined how she must look to the passing carriages full of dry passengers—a runaway bride, soaked to the bone.

Finally, out of breath, she reached the front stoop of the MacLeod house and prayed that she was right in assuming Drummond would be there. She banged on the door, wildly knocking and becoming more anxious with each passing moment of resounding silence. There she stood, in a sodden wedding dress, a mass of wilted blooms in her hair, about to give up all hope of future happiness, when the door swung open.

"Penelope, what the hell are ye doin' here?" Drummond's jaw hung open and he rubbed at his eyes as if he couldn't believe what he saw before him.

"Drummond, I couldn't do it. I had to come," she announced in a rush. Penelope longed to touch him, to fall into his arms. And she would have, if she knew how he would receive her. But judging by the look on his face, he would be too stunned to catch her.

"It *is* ye." His voice was barely a whisper and he swore something in Gaelic, looking from side to side down the rainy lanes before grabbing her arm and pulling her inside. He slammed the door behind them and took a deep breath before turning to face her. "Christ, Penelope, ye'll catch your death runnin' about like that!"

"I know, but I couldn't get a carriage," she said, feeling the distance between them. She looked down, watching the water from her dress spread onto the oriental carpet, darkening it beneath her feet.

Drummond looked her up and down from the top of her blossom filled hair to the soggy hem of her wedding gown. "I see congratulations are in order, aye?"

"Hardly. I'm betting that my mother is about to die from disappointment and my father is dead because she has killed him in the middle of the church."

"So ye are no' married?" he asked calmly, obviously still in a slight state of shock. "Did ye run from your own weddin', then?"

"I did. I had to."

"But I thought ye loved him?"

Penelope's mouth gaped open. "*Loved* him? Where on God's green earth did you get a ridiculous idea like that?"

"Ye got engaged and almost married." He began pacing the length of the entryway, not looking her way. "What else should a man think?

"Well, firstly, *you* left *me*," she retorted, wagging a finger at him. "Secondly, I had to marry him to save my father's business." Penelope sniffed a bit, beginning to shiver in her wet silks. "He's going under and we have no money to save it. Marrying Theodore would have saved everything, but I couldn't go through with it. Well, I would have, had I not seen you on the road earlier. Seeing you was a sign that I was making a mistake."

"Ye gave up that, your family's livelihood, for me?" His voice had a slight hitch to it.

"My parents will be fine, they always are. But I wouldn't be, had I married him today. I'd give up anything to be with you." She took a deep breath before uttering the words she had spoken only in private. "*Mo anam buin ri sibh.*"

"My soul belongs to ye." Drummond's eyes softened and he drew her against his chest, wrapping his massive arms around her. They stayed like that for a while before Penelope noticed his shirt becoming damp. "Christ," he muttered, pulling away. "Ye can no' go around in this drenched dress. Ye'll freeze."

"It's not like I packed a bag when I ran from the church," she said with a light laugh, attempting to ease the mood, which was still tense and awkward. Or, at least, she felt it was so.

He put an arm around her shoulder and began leading her to the stairs. "Come. I know Charlotte would no' mind ye borrowin' somethin' to wear."

As soon as she had pulled a dressing robe from her friend's closet, she turned to Drummond who was leaving, closing the bedroom door to give her privacy. "Wait."

"What is it?"

"I can't undress myself." Her words were true. It took two maids to sew her into the gown, specially made for her in Paris. She had no idea how she was going to get the cursed frock off.

"Now is no' the time." He ran his hand through his hair, looking away from her. "I've seen ye unbutton a dress before."

"This dress has no buttons," Penelope told him, unpinning her veil from her head and tossing it to the floor. "It needs to be cut off."

"Cut off?" He furrowed his brow before shrugging and passing her the dirk at his hip.

Penelope clutched the blade, surprised at its weight. "I can't do it myself. I'll miss and puncture a kidney." She handed it back to him and resumed plucking the blossoms from her hair.

"Ye can no' expect me to really slice open your weddin' dress?"

"Unless you want me to freeze, you must."

He grimaced, holding the knife gingerly. "It does no' feel right…almost sacrilegious. Ye came from your weddin' to another man and now I'll be the one to undress ye."

"I'm not married," she reminded him softly. "By now my father has told everyone that I've fled and it'll be the talk of the ton by sundown. You helping me out of this dress is the least of my worries."

"Ye've come clean to your father?"

"Yes. He didn't know that I was marrying for money, but once I told him about us, he said he understood."

"He knows we are…were involved?"

"To an extent…." Penelope paused, wondering how much of the story she should tell him, but decided it was for the best that he knew it all. "You see, Theodore was *involved* with his maid."

"The bastard," he growled, looking back up at her. "He did no' know what he had."

"And he never will."

Drummond regarded her for a moment then cleared his throat. “Do ye mean…ye and him never…ye did no’…”

“We were never intimate, if that’s what you mean.” Penelope hating having to say it out loud but knew that it needed to be done, no matter how awkward.

“I…I’m no’ ashamed to say that I’m happy to hear it.”

She shifted in her heavy gown. “Now, please, help me out of this so we can talk more. I’m going to catch my death.”

Drummond came to her and held the back of her gown, pulling it away from her body in order to slip the edge of the blade at the silk above her tailbone. In one smooth motion he sliced the dress open. “Is that enough to get it off?”

“Yes,” she told him as the gooseflesh prickled upon the exposed skin, slightly disappointed that he didn’t undress her further. But, she knew that she shouldn’t expect too much too quickly. They had a lot more to discuss.

“Penelope, what will ye do now?” he asked, his gaze politely averted.

She turned to face him, clenching the bodice of her gown to keep it from falling. “I don’t rightly know. I haven’t thought past what would happen once I found you, and even that was a gamble I hadn’t thought through.”

“Think about it before ye burn your bridges. I do no’ want to se ye hurt.” Drummond brushed his fingers against her cheek before leaving the room, giving her privacy to change.

Left alone, Penelope dropped the sodden silks to the ground and dragged it into the bathroom. She wrapped the robe around herself and checked her face in the mirror. A laugh threatened to burst from her mouth when she saw how her perfectly curled bun had deflated, leaving her with a sopping mop upon her head.

No wonder Drummond was uninterested in her reappearance. While he seemed happy to see her, he didn't appear exalted as she hoped he would. Their meeting was awkward and unromantic and she began to wonder if she made a mistake. If Drummond rebuffed her, she would be left scandalized for nothing. But at least in her old age, a spinster in one of her brother's homes, she could tell her masses of adopted cats how she did anything she could for love. Charming.

No matter the consequences, she had to see things through. The house was still silent as she left the bedroom to find Drummond. She peeked in each doorway as she passed them, stopping only when she saw him seated upon a bed in one of the smaller guest rooms. His hands were clasped between his knees and his eyes were fixed upon the floor. He seemed to be deep in thought.

"Drummond, may I come in?" Penelope asked from the hall.

"Aye." He nodded, glancing up at her.

Tentatively, she entered, closing the door behind her and sat on the edge of the mattress, a mere foot away from him. "Over the shock yet?" she inquired, half joking and half serious.

"No, and I do no' think I ever will be."

Penelope hated the thought of baring her soul to him but knew she must if she had a chance at keeping him. "I thought you would be happy to see me."

He brought his eyes up to meet her gaze. "I *am* happy to see you. I thought I'd never do so again. I just do no' know what to do now, or what to think. Ye left your betrothed for me. I would have never asked ye to do such a thing. Especially when ye made such a fair match."

"A fair match?" Penelope knew that he looked down on soft-handed British men with their delicate interests and aloof mannerisms. She couldn't believe he would think one of them was a good counterpart for her.

"Aye. He's a well-off man with a verra good reputation. Your family adores him and I know they were pleased with the pairin'. Hell, everyone knew." Drummond looked away and ran a hand through his hair. "They'd never be pleased if it were me who came to call."

Penelope's chest tightened and she bridged the distance between them, planting a hand on his arm and giving the muscles a reassuring squeeze. "*I* would be and that's all that matters." She waited for him to look at her again, but he didn't.

"I'm no good for ye, Penelope. I do no' know how to live in British society. I only know how to fight and ride."

"And to love." Penelope cupped his face, forcing it to turn. "I've never met anyone like you. I don't want someone from a fine English family who wears powdered gloves and talks of nothing but flowers. I want an honest, hard-working Scot. I want *you*."

His emerald eyes searched her face. "Do ye mean that, truly?"

"I do."

Drummond grabbed her face, pulling her lips to his. "God, I love ye more than ye know."

Penelope collapsed onto the bed with Drummond close behind. Her heart hammered wildly as they tore at each other's clothes, wordlessly expressing their need for supreme closeness. Penelope was naked beneath her robe, having left her shift and corset in the bathroom with her broken vows. When Drummond's hands deftly undid the tie at her waist, he paused.

"If we go further, I do no' know if I could stop myself from havin' ye," he whispered, stroking the thin line of her collarbone with a finger, eyes upon her face and not her nude form.

"I don't want to stop." She brought her hands to his belt and unbuckled the strip of leather. "We *won't* stop. Not this time."

He fell upon her again, his mouth hungrily engulfing her breast, his tongue swirling around the sensitive peak. Penelope clasped his head to her chest. Her mind rambled on with impure thoughts of their unholy union. She knew she should blush, stop their physical joining, but she was also sure that she was where she was meant to be—in Drummond's arms.

He pulled his shirt over his head before removing Penelope's open robe. He helped her pull her arms free, leaving her completely bare before him. She heard him mutter something in muted Gaelic and she ran her own hands down his torso, feeling the curvature of each well-defined muscle. While she had touched him before, everything still felt so new. There was nothing to stop them and they had all the time in the world.

Penelope urged him to touch her at the juncture of her thighs, which was now slick with her arousal. But, he took his time, his fingers lazily tracing each slope and swell of her body. Her skin alighted with each passing brush. But no matter how she wriggled and arched, he carefully avoided the one spot that so desperately needed him.

"Please hurry," she gasped when his teeth grazed a nipple.

He glanced up at her with smirk, his tousled russet hair hanging before his eyes. "There's no rush."

"I've been waiting for too long." Penelope tried to sound forceful but her words came out a strangled whisper when his fingers lightly touched her sex, sending shivers down her spine.

He began a gentle exploration of her folds. With each tender caress, Penelope begged louder for him to join with her, to allow them both some release. But each time, she was rewarded with nothing more than a soft kiss upon her lips. She longed for him to enter her, to fill the empty void she didn't know was there before she met him.

"Are ye sure ye want me to do this?" he asked in a hush.

Penelope looed deeply into his eyes and could almost see the desire in them, the unbridled lust he was trying to contain. "I'm sure," she replied, feeling the edge of his kilt, the only barrier between them. "I've never been so positive of anything before in my life. I know what I want."

"Penelope," Drummond said, bringing his face close and holding her against him, his hands stopping their playful ministration. "Once this is done, there'll be no goin' back for ye. Ye'll no longer be a maid."

"I don't want to go back. I chose you, Drummond. I want you, not only in bed, but in life." She palmed his angular face, tracing his bottom lip with her thumb, enjoying its fullness. "I'd rather be your poor wife in Scotland than anyone else's rich wife anywhere in the world."

He swallowed and cupped her cheek with his palm, his eyes still trained on hers. "Ye might no' be my first, but I'll have ye as my last. I'll cherish ye every day if ye agree to be mine."

"I've been yours." She held up her right hand, showing him the Scottish amethysts. "I'll *always* be yours. That will never change for me."

He kissed the stones before moving above her, gently parting her thighs. His manhood rubbed against her opening, making her moan with primal desire, and slightly with fear of what was yet to come. Penelope grabbed at his muscular lower back as he towered over her, ready for him to take her. The longing to truly be his, in every sense of the word, was unbelievably overwhelming.

Drummond eased himself into her, each staggering inch satisfying her hunger. When he was fully sheathed within her, Penelope cried out for him to go on, the pain of her maidenhead tearing soon replaced with the demand to continue their sinful joining. He murmured Scottish in her ear as he slowly thrust inside her, his manhood effortlessly moving within her wet core.

Penelope let the erotic friction of their coupling carry her away and she felt the buildup of pleasure with each rigid stroke. She dragged her nails down the curve of his spine as the tidal wave of pleasure crashed down around her. Drummond let go as well, emptying his seed within her, fully consummating their love with a final act of claiming.

He fell beside her, his chest heaving with exertion and clutched her hand, pressing his lips upon her palm. "Are ye all right?"

"Yes," she said, curling into his body, smiling in sleepy contentment.

"I love ye, Penelope."

"And I, you." She sighed, burrowing deeper into his chest.

The deed was done and now no one could try to force her to marry anyone, no matter their financial standing. As a "ruined" woman, no man would dare take her on, especially knowing her claimer was a giant Scot with arms as big as their torsos and a blade at his hip. She giggled a bit at the thought of the ton gasping at Drummond joining her at the next ball as her open suitor…perhaps even her husband.

"What's so funny?"

She picked the wayward pins that dug into her scalp from her hair. "It's nothing. I'm just happy."

He gave her a tight squeeze and kissed the top of her head. "Aye, me, as well."

When a sharp knock sounded at the bedroom door, Penelope startled, diving to the floor to retrieve her borrowed dressing gown. "Who is that?"

Drummond shrugged and took his time haphazardly rearranging the kilt that still clung to his hips. He opened the door to reveal a nervous-looking maid. "Yes?"

"There are some people here to see you. They say it's very pressing that you speak," the maid said, her gaze darting away from a freshly bedded Penelope.

"Who is it?" Drummond asked.

"I believe is Baron and Baroness Elmsly." The maid dipped a short curtsey before darting away.

Penelope knew that the maids usually weren't so flighty, as they saw all the gory and humiliating inner workings of the best households. Her eagerness to remove herself probably meant there would be hell to pay when they descended from Drummond's chambers. Her mind began to race as she contemplated their next move. While her father might have been understanding in the moment, the reality of Theodore's money no longer keeping the business afloat may have hit him, causing him to change his mind. And she was certain her mother held ill will toward them both for depriving her of a wealthy son-in-law and constant cash inflow. Penelope could imagine her parents seething in the entryway.

Drummond pulled his shirt back on, his square jaw firmly set. "I suppose we have to go see what they have to say."

"It won't be anything good," she mumbled, taking a glance in the looking glass. She tried to suppress her wayward hair, but the tendrils were sufficiently mussed. Penelope took the rest of the pins out, hoping it would make her look a bit more presentable, but it did not have the desired effect.

"They won't try to force ye home, or into marriage, will they?" he asked worriedly.

The thought chilled her but, then she remembered her ace card. "They can't."

"They are still your parents and they may try. It is their right, after all," he pointed out, buckling his belt. "It would no' come to that, though, as I'd never let them take ye from me. But all the same, I'll have ye as my bride as soon as I'm able, to ensure nothin' happens."

"We've had carnal knowledge of each other," she murmured, tapping her chip thoughtfully. She was wondering how fast her mother would swoon at the thought of her only daughter having been bedded. Cecily might even keel over and perish in the entryway, but not without a few choice words.

"Aye, but it's no' as if ye can just go down there and tell them I've had ye." He laughed dryly before noting Penelope's serious demeanor. "That's no what ye are thinkin' o' doin', is it?"

"And what if I did?"

"Your father might punch me, and I'd deserve it and take it like a man. All the same, I've seen people lie all the time. There's no reason why they would no' lie about ye still bein' a maid in order to find ye a new match. Would it really be enough to ensure they do no' try to take ye?

Penelope held herself up to her full, but still diminutive, height. "I'd like to see them try." Sounding braver than she felt, she tied her robe tighter around her, leaving the bedroom and going to the top of the staircase.

"What are ye doin'? Drummond asked, gripping her arm. "Ye are no' dressed!"

"That's the point." She fluffed her hair and began her descent, her blood rushing to her ears and her meager breakfast threatening to make an appearance. "Just trust me."

Her parents stood in the entryway. Edmund looked exhausted while Cecily was openly sobbing, keening to the heavens, asking how she raised such a wild girl who hated her so, despite all of her loving efforts. When they caught sight of a scantily clad Penelope, both took a sharp intake of breath.

"Penelope! What on earth are you wearing?" Cecily looked fit to faint and began fanning herself violently, her hand clutching the bannister.

Edmund cleared his throat, his eyes averted. "Darling, don't you have something less…*revealing* to wear?"

"Not to be crass, but I didn't have much time to dress." Penelope glanced at her mother, gauging her reaction.

"Penelope, no," Cecily croaked. "Tell me you *didn't*!"

"I did, and I'd do it again! In fact, I can promise you that I will."

"Ooh!" Cecily swooned, slowly so as to not hurt herself, but loudly, to emit the most sympathy from her uninterested audience.

Penelope rolled her eyes. "Mother, please, let's all be adults."

Cecily opened one eye from her spot on the oriental carpet, still damp from Penelope's entrance. "Why has God cursed me with such a wonton for a daughter?" She cried out again and threw her fan over her face. "What grievous sin have I committed?

"Should I call for some tea, then?" Drummond interrupted. He sat on the step behind Penelope, watching the proceedings with interest. No one had noticed him until then.

Edmund looked around Penelope. "I take it you're the Drummond MacGregor I've heard about?"

"Aye." He stood, passing her to shake Edmund's hand. "Pleased to meet ye, although I wish it were under better circumstances."

"As do I." Edmund crouched down next to his wife, who peered at him through half-open eyes.

"Doesn't *anyone* care that I'm dying of a broken heart?" Cecily sounded more annoyed than upset.

Penelope's father sighed and held out a hand. "Come, dear, let's go have a nice cup of tea. I do believe we all have a lot to discuss."

***

Penelope thought the foursome was an uncomfortable bunch, indeed. Cecily still lamented the loss of her newest son, loudly crying into her handkerchief. Edmund sat stoically beside his wife, sipping his tea, looking as awkward as he probably felt. And poor Drummond sat at a distance from Penelope, obviously not wishing to remind her parents that he had just bedded her. Perhaps they should have called for a stronger drink than tea.

"So," Edmund cut through the silence, putting his teacup on the side table, "where do we start?"

"I suppose the beginnin'," Drummond said.

"Well, I think it's only right that I'm the one to tell this particular tale." Penelope fingered the tie of her robe. "Drummond and I became acquainted at Charlotte's wedding."

"I knew she was trouble!" Cecily wailed. "She ran off with a Scot first, and now you are going down the same twisted path!"

She ignored her mother. "At first I merely offered to help him write a book about MacGregor legends and songs. It was business to begin with. We wanted to preserve the art of his clan."

"Wait a moment," Edmund cut in enthusiastically, "are you to tell me that you've penned that book all my customers are fighting over? The blue covered one with the songs?"

Drummond gave a noncommittal shoulder raise. "Aye. Penelope wrote the music for it all. And the English bits where it was needed. And compiled it. In fact, she did more than her fair share."

"I was just getting there," Penelope said, slightly annoyed at the constant interruptions. She felt as if she needed to get the entire story out, or she would explode. "As I was explaining, we began working at the book together and, as we continued to meet, feelings began to grow between us, although we tried to dismiss them many times."

"Why didn't you ever say anything before? Certainly we could have all met and done without the whole…wedding matter." Edmund sighed. "This may have all been avoided without all the terrible losses."

Drummond shook his head. "I am no' a lord or duke, or have a fancy title and lands."

"No lands," Cecily moaned.

"I had verra little to offer her when we met and she did no' want to disappoint ye. We both knew that our marriage would bring nothin' but sorrow to ye both."

"And Theodore, dear Theodore and all his beautiful ships!" Cecily wiped her eyes. "I don't understand."

"It was never about Theodore." Penelope sighed. "I settled for him because Drummond left and I thought that it was for the best to marry well and be done with it."

"It was!" Fresh tears streamed down her mother's face. "He was handsome, moneyed, the perfect gentleman, and could have saved the Piccadilly Emporium!"

Penelope felt anger fester in her belly. "Mother, you can't just sell me off. Theodore didn't love me like Drummond does, and I didn't love him. I never did and I never could. You always told me you would allow me to marry for love."

Edmund put a hand on his wife's arm. "She's right, Cecily. We couldn't put a price on her happiness."

"Penelope!" Someone shouted, and they heard clicking heels on the marble floors. "Drummond, where are you?"

"In here!" Drummond called out.

Panting, Flora burst through the doors of the drawing room, resting her hands on her knees, trying to catch her breath. "Your parents are on their way! Came as fast as I could…you need to get a carriage!" When she saw Penelope's parents, her face glowed red and her mouth dropped open.

"Hello, Flora." Drummond nodded his head, the corners of his mouth twitching in amusement. "Ye remember the Baron and the Baroness?"

"Good to see you," Flora squeaked.

Charlie's red head popped in beside Flora, his eyes sparkling with mirth. "Lovely to see you, Baron Elmsly, Madam." His gaze wandered to Penelope and Drummond. "Oh, my word."

"Charlie, how nice to see you," Penelope said awkwardly. She knew he would be highly amused by all the delicious gossip."

"Pleasure, as always." Charlie nodded. "Charming dressing robe. Top notch."

Flora elbowed him roughly in the side before pushing him back from the doorway. "We'll just excuse ourselves." She slipped away, closing the door behind her.

"The Scottish," Cecily mumbled. "Why couldn't you have run away with a duke or marquis?"

"I'm sorry I didn't select a partner that suited your desires, Mother," Penelope huffed, crossing her arms over her chest and slumping down in her seat.

"Why didn't you think about your poor father and I? We're practically destitute!" She tossed her handkerchief onto the floor.

Edmund gathered his wife in his arms. "We'll make it through—sell the arcade, maybe the country home. By the time we liquidate our assets, we'll be out of the hole. It'll all be set right, never fear."

"It's twenty thousand *pounds*, Edmund! We'll never be able to scrape it together."

Penelope shifted uncomfortably, feeling guilty about throwing away her parents' business. It was never her intention to fail them, but she also couldn't fail herself. The decision was made as soon as she stepped foot out of the church and there was no going back. She saw Drummond move, drawing himself up and making a silent exit from the room. She bit her lip, wondering if he was overwhelmed by her mother's negativity. Her heart beat loudly against her breastbone.

"What now?" Cecily hissed, yanking her fan from her bag and flapping it madly once again. "Are you going to abandon us to go live on a-a-a *farm* like some sort of *fishwife*?"

"So, what if I was?" Penelope asked. "Drummond's a good man and he loves me. Why isn't that enough for you?"

"You're the daughter of a baron. You could have any man you wanted in England." Cecily patted her bun, obviously getting over the emotional dramatics. "And yet all you got was a Scottish man with no money and no prospects!"

"No, I got the man that I wanted," she told her mother, thrusting out her hand to show off her Scottish amethysts. "I'm going to be with Drummond no matter that you say. No other man will take me now, especially when it's possible that I'm *pregnant*."

Cecily paled, her eyes widening. "Pregnant? No. You can't be. I refuse it!"

"Mother, you know how children come to be. You've had several. Right now I could be carrying a Scottish baby." Penelope patted her flat stomach, watching as her mother floundered for words. But as harsh as it was, she knew it needed to be said. Drummond had claimed her mind, body, and soul. After their bedroom romp, it was quite possible for her to be with child very soon. The thought warmed her and set a fluttering through her chest.

Edmund cleared his throat, his ears pink. "Well, let's not get ahead of ourselves, now. If we're going to make things work, then we need to come to an understanding. Penelope, you know that we don't have the funds to support you, a husband, and any children you might have. When business was good, maybe, but now…there's no way we could give you the money to live the life you are accustomed to."

"And you won't need to," Penelope said firmly. "Drummond owns a small bit of land and is one of Conner's top warriors."

"That's the plan then?" Edmund sighed. "If that's what you want, then we will accept it."

"Pardon me." Drummond stood in the doorway, his face unreadable. "I'd like to give ye somethin'."

Edmund shook his head. "Oh, no, dear boy. You don't have to give us anything."

"I do. Consider it an act o' good faith that I'll care for your daughter in the way she deserves to be cared for from this moment on." Drummond held out a slip of paper, passing it to Edmund.

Penelope craned her neck to see what it was, but she was too far away. "What is it?"

Edmund clutched his chest, his mouth agape. "Where did you…how did you? I can't accept this. It's too grand."

"Let me see." Cecily snatched the paper, her lips moving rapidly as her eyes scanned the words. "How can it be?"

Penelope grew impatient. "Will someone *please* tell me what's going on?"

"Mister MacGregor is paying off our debts," Edmund whispered. He sounded as if he was in shock.

"How is that possible?" Penelope asked, looking to Drummond for answers.

"The book sells well," Drummond said with a shrug. "Between the royalties, the advance for the second, and the plot o' my land that pulls a fine harvest, I've come into a bit o' money these past few months I've been gone from London."

"How well?" she questioned, this time looking toward her mother.

"Thirty. Thousand. Pounds." Cecily's voice was barely a whisper as she spoke.

Penelope stood, crossing the room to Drummond. Her mind was swimming with thoughts. "I don't understand. Why give them the money? It's more than they even need! How will we live? Why didn't you tell me?"

"Those are a lot o' questions." Drummond laughed, sitting beside her on the couch. "Well, I give them the money because I can, because I want to, and because I need to show that I'm no' some poor Scottish fool who will drag their daughter down to the gutter."

Penelope opened her mouth to protest but he silenced her with a look. "As to your other questions, we'll live in London in the townhome I just purchased, during the season, as ye like it. In the summers, my simple house in Scotland is bein' added on to so as to give us some more room. And we'll always have a place in the MacLeod castle so ye could see Charlotte whenever ye pleased. As for me no' tellin' ye, I did no' have the time." He dipped down so only she could hear the next words that passed his lips. "As ye might remember, we were otherwise engaged."

"You have the means to just *give* us thirty thousand pounds?" Cecily was still staring up at him, stunned beyond belief.

Drummond nodded. "Aye. If ye need more, I'll have to go to the bank on the morrow. I believe my account only allows me to write notes for thirty thousand at a time."

Penelope gazed up at Drummond's face, wondering how she got so lucky to find such a man to love. Certainly they could have gone about their romance better, but the end result was just as perfect, if not more so, than she thought possible. She got the man she desired, her father could keep the Piccadilly Emporium, and she knew her future was ensured.

Cecily stood, smiling in a way that surprised them all. "Come, my son," she crooned, her arms open wide, "give Mother a hug."

Epilogue

Penelope stood in the small stone chapel on the MacLeod lands, looking out at the rolling green hills from her dressing room window. The early fall air was crisp and clean, wafting in, cooling her in her bridal gown. She was thankful for the breeze, as her nerves made her feel rather hot and stifled.

"Penelope, may I come in?" Charlotte asked, opening the door a crack.

She turned, smiling as her friend entered, a basket tucked in the crook of her arms and a bundle in her hands. "Charlotte, I'm so glad you're here. I couldn't finish dressing for my wedding without you."

"Especially since I've brought the heather."

Penelope went to her, peeking in at the blankets, gazing down to the angelic face of the newest MacLeod. "And how is baby Alec?"

"Finally asleep. The little man isn't the easier to soothe, sometimes. Now, sit down so I might do your hair and you can hold the baby. I'll need my hands free."

Penelope cradled the little boy, watching as his rosebud lips opened and shut in a dream-like state. "He is a handsome little thing."

"He is." Charlotte began picking the pins from Penelope's hair.

"What are you doing?"

"You're in Scotland now, marrying a Scottish man. You'll look like a Scottish bride."

"So this is why you've brought the baby—so I can't fight you off?"

Charlotte grinned, draping the loose locks around Penelope's face. "You know me so well. But, I must ask, this isn't the same wedding dress you left Theodore Harrison in, is it?"

Penelope laughed. "Goodness, no! I bought this off the rack at my father's store. It's not as if I had the time to get a specially made dress from Paris again. Mother wanted me married off straight away."

"With this fine lace and low neckline, I don't think Drummond will have a problem with it not being designed just for you."

"How funny this is," she said, watching Charlotte as she braided heather and orange blossoms into her hair, making a leafy crown.

"What?"

"Before your own wedding, I was helping you dress when, all the while, you were plotting like a little sneak to get Drummond and I together. And now, here I am, you assisting me as I go to meet him at the altar."

"I know you better than anyone and I knew you wouldn't do with some silly fop with powdered gloves, as much as you claimed."

"You do." Penelope carefully dislodged one hand from under the sleeping babe, placing it upon one of Charlotte's. "Thank you, truly, for bringing him to me."

"Oh, posh," Charlotte giggled, pinning a sheer veil to Penelope's floral crown.

Penelope handed Alec back to Charlotte, looking forward to a time when she could hold her own child in her arms. Drummond had gone to the Highlands ahead of her, to prepare their Scottish home for the start of their married life, and Penelope couldn't wait to get her hands on him. The idea of him cradling his own child brought tears to her eyes.

"Oh, don't start to cry!" Charlotte's voice warbled. "If you start, then I'll start, and then Alec will start, and the morning will be spoiled."

Penelope laughed, brushing away the tears. "Then let's get me to the altar before we both fall apart."

She grabbed her bouquet of roses, heather, and orange blossoms, gripping them tightly to control the shaking of her hands. While Penelope wasn't nervous for married life, the trembling came from the poignant excitement she felt. In less than an hour she would be not an English miss, but a Scottish wife to the finest man she had ever know. Drummond had practically rushed her to marriage and, for that, she was grateful. He had planned the entire ceremony, only asking that she come as soon as she was able.

Charlotte left Penelope with Baron Elmsly,

going in to take her seat.

"Dear, you look marvelous," Edmund muttered with a sigh. "I've never seen a more perfect bride."

"Thank you." Penelope peeked into the church. "Is it time yet?"

Edmund chuckled. "So eager! Thank goodness."

"I am. I really just want to marry him, Father."

"Then let's go." He held out an arm, knocking on the door of the church to call the harpist's attention to begin the "Wedding March."

Penelope could hear her heart thumping against her breastbone and wondered, as she entered the church, if the guests could hear it, too. She peered through her veil at Drummond, but the fabric made him hazy and hard to make out. But she could spot his towering, red and black tartan-clad figure in any crowd. She hoped he was as happy as she.

When the pair passed Cecily at the front of the aisle, her mother let out a shrill wail of glee at seeing her daughter a bride. A stern Charlotte, who pointed to the baby in her lap, hushed the sound and the woman's cries turned to quiet sobs, muted by a handkerchief pressed to her lips. Flora, who sat to her left, grinned widely, dramatically clasping her hands together and causing a short giggle to fall from Penelope's lips.

"Who gives this woman to be married?" the priest asked.

"I do," Edmund replied, lifting Penelope's veil and kissing her cheek before going to join Cecily in the pew.

Penelope finally turned to Drummond who looked more handsome than she thought possible, standing tall before his family and friends. He grinned widely, his vibrantly green eyes sending chills up her spine as he took in her gown, and the bare skin it displayed. Charlotte hopped up, taking Penelope's wedding bouquet to free her from the cumbersome bunch.

The priest cleared his throat before beginning. "Before the four points o' the Earth. Before the sun, the wind, the air, the water, the ground. Before the people o' England and the people o' the clans. Before the God and the ancient ones that came before. This man and this woman are enterin' into the bonds of matrimony to become one mind, one soul, one body, one heart."

Penelope started, confused. She'd never heard a priest speak such vows before. But as she gazed up at Drummond, his expression one of pure, open love, she assumed what was taking place was something perfectly commonplace in Scotland. She was, as Charlotte had told her, a Scottish bride.

Drummond took her hands in his, his right with her right and his left with her left, their interlaced arms making a cross. He gripped her fingers in reassurance. "We'll be havin' a symbolic hand fastin'," Drummond whispered. "A blendin' o' two worlds, aye?"

Penelope nodded, not taking her eyes off of her future husband.

"Drummond MacLeod MacGregor, do ye enter into this hand fastin', and o' this marriage, of your own free will, for no' the entirety o' a year and a day, but for the rest o' this life and the next?" the priest asked seriously, taking a length of MacGregor plaid from the altar.

"I do," Drummond answered.

The old priest turned to her. "Penelope Katherine Elmsly, do ye enter into this hand fastin', and o' this marriage, of your own free will, for no' the entirety o' a year and a day, but for the rest o' this life and the next?

"I do." Her voice was barely more than a breath.

He addressed Drummond, winding the strip of tartan tightly around their clasped hands. "Do ye promise to live for this woman as your true wife, forsakin' all others?"

"I do."

The old man wound the cloth in another ring. "Do ye promise to live for this man as your true husband, forsakin' all others?"

"I do."

"Do ye promise on sword and life to protect and provide for this woman and all those who come from this union?" the priest asked Drummond. "To fight, reap, and sow in her honor?"

"I do."

He held the final piece of plaid and turned to Penelope. "Do ye promise on home and hearth to care and provide for this man and all those who come from this union? To bear bairns, reap, and sow in his honor?"

"I do." Penelope held in a cry of happiness as the fabric was knotted firmly over their hands, signifying the finality of their union.

"Now ye are as husband and wife in this life, and the next. Live in God's love and may your marriage be as strong as the bond that now ties ye together."

He took their hands and smoothly drew each from the tartan, incredibly keeping the knot securely tied. "Now MacGregor will give her the ring and the colors o' his name."

Drummond pulled a gold band from his sporran. "Penelope, I stand before ye as your husband, vowing to love ye, care for ye, and give ye the home and family ye deserve. I'm luckier than most to have found a wife so kind and beautiful who saw me as a good investment for, God knows, ye've a good lot o' work before ye."

"I love you just as you are," Penelope promised as the wedding band encircled her left ring finger. She welcomed the new addition.

The priest stepped back and Conner took his place, holding a large piece of MacGregor plaid. Drummond stared at Penelope, not breaking their gaze, and took the fabric from his hand. Tenderly he brushed the blonde curls away from her right shoulder before putting the tartan over it.

Once again reaching into his sporran, Drummond produced a silver pin. It was a delicate thing of two intertwined hearts, topped with a crown that held five small amethysts at their peaks. She recognized it as a Luckenbooth broach—the sign of a newly married woman. He fastened it to the two sides of the plaid, fixing them upon her left hip. She stroked the soft fabric, loving the feel of the MacGregor colors against her skin.

Drummond and Penelope drew together, finally a wedded pair with nothing to separate them. Penelope eyed her husband, devastatingly handsome with strong arms to hold, and protect her, from all they would face. When their lips met to indicate the beginning of their married life, Penelope felt a sense of peace and warmth wash over her. The feeling magnified when Drummond pulled her to his chest, burying his face in her flower-filled hair.

"*Mo anam buin ri sibh*," he murmured, his voice filled with emotion.

Penelope smiled. "My soul belongs to you."

About the Author

Kelsey McKnight is a university-educated historian from southern New Jersey. She has married her great loves of romance, history, and literature to create her first works that are set in Scotland. But she has recently begun to venture into the world of contemporary romance, drawing inspiration from true life. When she's not writing, Kelsey can be found reading, drinking too much coffee, blogging, spending time with her family, and working for two separate nonprofit organizations.

Facebook:
Facebook.com/Kissatmidnight

Twitter:
Twitter.com/KelseyMMcK

Website:
Kissatmidnight.wordpress.com

Instagram:
Instagram.com/akissatmidnight

Goodreads:
Goodreads.com/Kelsey_McKnight

www.ingramcontent.com/pod-product-compliance
Lightning Source LLC
Chambersburg PA
CBHW030326200626
46816CB00006BA/1944

* 9 7 8 1 6 4 0 3 4 1 2 3 4 *